SOUL OF A MAN

CURRIE ALEXANDER POWERS

Cover design by Karen Powers for Powerhouse!!! Inc.
Cover photo and author photo by Cheryl Powers

Printed in the United States of America
ISBN 1-58385-081-3

This book is for Colin

ACKNOWLEDGEMENTS

I would like to thank the following people:

My family; Marian Alexander Powers, who taught me the art of storytelling, Karen Powers and Cheryl Powers for starting Powerhouse!!! Inc. so they could design the beautiful cover for this book, Robert Powers for loving books and being a damn fine architect, and my late father, Robert George Powers for giving me my first tool box and teaching me that an idea can be made into something real.

I'd also like to thank my writing buddies from CAPS; Kathy Rhodes, Colleen Speroff, Susie Dunham, Chance Chambers, and Kristin Tubb, who helped me with the spelling of American words, and without whom I could not have finished this book.

I'd also like to thank those who encouraged me to write; David Hayes, Bruce Cockburn, Evelyn Linden, Suzanne Kingsbury, and Ray Bonneville

Thanks to James Lee Burke whose eloquent words have inspired me over and over again

Thanks to the wonderful people of Peterborough, Ontario; Curtis, Barbara, Joe, Luke; I hope they don't mind the liberties I took with their town

Thanks to the musicians whose music keeps my heart beating; Howlin' Wolf, Blackie & The Rodeo Kings, Lucinda Williams, Edvard Grieg, Peter Gabriel, and Blind Willie Johnson for writing Soul of a Man so I could borrow the title

And most importantly, thanks to my husband, Colin Linden, who liked hearing me read out loud, and whose love and faith led me on, through the storm, through the night.

SOUL OF A MAN

CURRIE ALEXANDER POWERS

Won't somebody tell me
Answer if you can
Won't somebody tell me
Tell me what is the soul of a man

—Blind Willie Johnson 1930

CHAPTER ONE

Jezebel Looks In The Mirror

I go through this routine every morning; open eyes, sit up, get out of bed, walk to bathroom, face mirror over sink. There, I stare at my reflection and say my full name out loud.

Albertine Hannah.

I do this all before I'm fully awake. I have to. I have a fear of not identifying myself first thing in the morning. If one day, instead, I wake up and go make coffee first, I'll be committed to that other identity, the one everyone in Watson thinks I am. I will become Anne Hanes.

Sometimes I have nightmares about it. I wake up and forget to face the mirror as Albertine. Then I remember sometime later, in a flurry, in a jumble, the way time happens in dreams and I rush to the bathroom, but it's too late. I look in the mirror and I'm someone else. I've become Anne Hanes.

She doesn't look like me, not the way I see myself from the inside, where I still have the face I had two years ago, the wrinkle-free expressions of someone whose life had not yet been altered by transgression.

A few times, when I've had those dreams, I've gotten up in the middle of the night and gone to the bathroom and done my mirror ritual. It scares me, but it's become a compulsion.

Don't get me wrong. I was the one who made the choice to become Anne Hanes when I moved here a year ago. I escaped Toronto like Jezebel with a pack of wild dogs on my heels. I found refuge here in Watson, small town, small world, the wild dogs here uninterested in picking up the scent of an impostor.

Lately I've been afraid each morning when I look in the mirror that my face is actually changing. My cheeks look fatter. Could be all this good clean living. Could be stagnation. I've let my hair grow long, past my ears, a hairstyle I haven't worn since I was twelve. My roots are showing, proving my hair is not naturally black. My eyes scare me the most. I catch my reflection with a startled expression and I wonder if that's how I look most of the time, deer in the head-lights, escaped prisoner in the beam of a watchtower spotlight.

I used to like my face, constant and familiar, proof like a fingerprint, an extension of my heart, blood and bones – the casing over my soul.

My face is changing as though it needs to accommodate my new name, but I am still Albertine on the inside. And that's the problem.

Albertine is the one who took that picture. A lot of people didn't like that picture. It *offended* them. It offended them so much it's been destroyed, like a mad dog put down with a bullet to the brain. And after-wards they were still offended. Which of course makes me wonder, was it the photo that offended them? Or was it me, the photographer?

I am an icy river, an infected sliver, a piece of broken glass.

I'm twenty-nine years old, hiding out in a small town, stalled, abridged, waiting for the ax to fall. I'm not sure what scares me more, my past being exposed, or my future committed to a lie.

CHAPTER TWO

August's Little Bird

God, August is beautiful. I watch him in the vacant lot behind our building. He's down there taking pictures of Christian's dinosaurs. That's what I call them. They're really giant masses of scrap metal welded together. They're scattered all over the parking lot like a construction aftermath.

Christian calls them sculptures. Christian is a welder, though he tries to escape that identity.

August squats down to shoot the dinosaur from a low angle. I watch his back, his long black hair, straight and heavy like a horse's tail falling over his shoulder. Like Oriental hair. August isn't Oriental. He's half aboriginal. Ojibwe, I think. I'd ask him if it didn't seem personal in the way that *personal* becomes embarrassing when you are obsessing over a person.

He leans over on one elbow to get a lower shot. I imagine what he's seeing through the viewfinder, the sculpture looming overhead like an imposing building, skeletal and rusting.

I know why August wants to take this picture. We share a knowledge of photography. We have creative sight. I just wish we could take the same pictures.

August rolls over. He's stretched out fully on the ground on his stomach in the dirt. I guess this explains why he does his laundry so often.

I like that about him. He's not afraid to roll in the mud. He doesn't sling it either.

When I come back after refilling my coffee cup, he's rolled over on his back and is staring through the lens of his camera up at the sky. I look up at the sky through the window.

Watson is pretty damn beautiful in the fall. The sky is a deep aching blue that makes all the other colors look brilliant against it. The trees are an inferno, flames licking the sky in violent streaks of red, orange and yellow. Autumn is death. Summer is determined to go out with a bang, I guess.

That's what August is going for I see. He's shooting the sky through a canopy of autumn leaves.

I wish I could kill this ache inside me.

I've been in this town for almost a year. Time is moving forward.

When you think of yourself as someone without a past, you forget that removing one life doesn't mean you're not going to grow another. I wiped my history clean. I had to. Threw out the garbage and washed my hands. All for naught. Every second that passes creates new history. More garbage is accumulating behind me even as I stand here doing nothing.

I was afraid to look behind me when I left Toronto, which also made me afraid to look ahead. And look where I ended up. Damn if I haven't grown a new life. I have friends, a home, and even a substitute career. I've become a part of people's lives. I didn't count on them being so accepting. I said I was Anne Hanes from Vancouver and they believed me.

August has gotten up from the ground. Suddenly his head jerks and he looks at the sky. I mirror his movements. A swarm of starlings, tiny and black as insects, arcing across the parking lot, the dog whistle soprano of a communal chirp, gone as fast as the rush of a car on the highway.

I close my eyes, trying to capture the sensation of fleeing.

There's a sound next door in August's studio. A mechanical bird, a mechanical chirp.

I open my eyes. Everything's blurry.

I look out the window to see if August's still there.

He's walking away, over to the trees, his movements distant, like in a silent movie.

Then I hear it. The sound from last night. I remember now. It wasn't the cuckoo clock in August's studio. It wasn't the mechanical bird with the mechanical chirp.

It was the sound of a hand hitting flesh.

The high muffled cry that followed was worse. It was the sound of someone trying to hide pain.

Move past it. Quickly.

A bunch of artists live here in The Factory. There's me, Julie, August and Christian, who is also landlord liaison, maintenance man and social activities director. His studio is across the hall from mine on the second floor. August is next door to me. We share a wall.

We also have a darkroom on the second floor, an old maintenance room that Christian and August converted. Christian installed a red light above the door when I moved in so August and I would know if the other was in there working.

Julie runs her fabric design company on the ground floor. She's successful enough to have two studios, one to live, and one to work. The rest of us are scraping by. The presence of at least one legitimate business makes our landlord, Mr. Zion, less nervous. The Factory makes some people in Watson nervous. I've heard it referred to as "that commune". They remember the sixties too vividly, I guess.

The Factory sits between two vacant lots on Water Street. The back of our building borders the river, like the frayed edge of a painting where the color gets jagged. There's some abandoned railroad tracks running through our parking lot. It's just dirt out there, like they ran out of pavement.

The forest skirts the edge of the river like a tall green beard. It runs north four blocks to the city park, where it ends abruptly at the manicured grass, and the riverbanks turn into a sandy beach. The beach is our favorite spot to have barbecues.

My studio is one large room, four hundred square feet. The east side has a floor to ceiling window overlooking the back parking lot and the forest. From my bed at night, I watch the tops of the trees swaying against the sky like black hands stroking a wall of gray. The forest scares me. It's a black shadowy well with beckoning fingers, inviting me in, daring me to be brave. But fear is a perpetual obstacle that cannot be conquered once and done with. I'm Sisyphus, rolling that stupid rock up the hill over and over again.

My kitchen and living room are part of my work studio. My bedroom has no walls. I work where I live and live where I work.

I have the bare minimum of anything, a fridge, stove, couch, table, filing cabinet, bed. On good days I tell myself that I'm lucky to be unburdened by the clutter of material things. I'm rich with freedom.

On bad days, my studio feels lonely and too big.

I've reached a crossroads. Watson was supposed to be temporary. Well, not even temporary, 'cause it's not like I moved here with my next stop in mind. I was just trying to survive the aftermath of my career implosion, do a little phoenix act and see if I could rise from the ashes and simply get up every morning and breathe one breath at a time until my life healed.

But, I'm still looking over my shoulder like the dogs are still following Jezebel. I need to find purity again. I need a clean soul. Then it won't matter if I'm Anne or Albertine. I'll be free.

The sun has gone behind a cloud. The pines are projecting huge shadows across the parking lot. Where did August go?

Then I see his familiar figure, graceful movement like a deer that's just wandered out of the forest and my heart thumps a few extra beats.

I watch him for a few more minutes. He's lying down now, in his original spot, maybe asleep. The trees make shadows across his face. I go get another cup of coffee from the kitchen.

"Great light," I say, standing over August casting my shadow.

"Mother Nature never fails to deliver," he says.

He smiles when I hand him a cup of coffee. August's face has the simplicity of a blind person, an absence of self-awareness and vanity that comes from a life of staring at your reflection. He's still lying on his back in the dirt, his camera on the ground beside him. One of Christian's sculptures is casting a giant shadow "X" on the ground beside him.

"I wonder if Christian was counting on the rust," I say, sitting down beside him.

Christian calls this dinosaur *The Crucifix*. The crisscrossed metal girders have gone powdery and orange from the rain.

I have a memory flash of Toronto. I haven't had one in quite awhile. It's my car, burned out and blackened, in the alley behind my old studio.

"Looks like a satellite that fell out of the sky," August says.

His voice sounds lazy. The car memory floats away as if it weighs nothing.

He moves his arms, sweeping them in slow arcs around his body like he's making snow angels in the dirt. His green plaid Muskoka dinner jacket – which August can wear without looking like a musician from Seattle – has bits of crushed leaves on the elbows. The toes of his black work boots are scuffed brown like abraded skin. He has them neatly laced right up to the top.

August was raised by various families on the Curve Lake Indian Reserve north of here. He lived only briefly with his grandmother. His mother abandoned him at birth, too restless to stay in the arms of the reservation, perhaps needing to follow the enticing scent of the man from Ottawa who'd left her pregnant. He was born in the month of August and his grandmother, already old and frail, was reluctant to name him in the hopes that his mother would return. Neighbors and relatives, impatient for something to call him, started referring to him as 'that August baby'. His name found him as though fate and destiny wanted him to grow up to be venerable, a heartbeat away from saintliness.

August was communal property; shared, breast-fed at every available nipple, taken into every home for a month here, a year there, an older brother at times, sometimes the middle child, sometimes the youngest. He's described his childhood as loving and kind, yet I can't help thinking he was passed around like unclaimed baggage.

In his face I see the paradox, the untainted smile of a boy who gleaned treasures from scraps. He must be made of Teflon. The shit in his life has slid right off him. He's scarless, unmarked by life, projected through the cruel mistake of his birth to manhood in a dent-proof missile.

"So what are you doing today?" he asks, with his eyes still closed.

"Watching the paint peel."

I look away from studying him, up to the sky, concentrating on finding the view August was seeing a few minutes ago through the lens of his camera. All I see are the trees moving. I can't still them with my eye into a framed photograph.

"You want to try one?" he says.

This is something August does all the time. He'll offer his camera. I always decline. I can't stand the thought of his roll of film being interrupted by one of my shots. It has to be a continuous thing, each frame committed by his eye alone. I hate that he's so generous he can think of each shot as a separate piece. I can't. A roll of film is like a mood that exists for a period of time and then it's over. The weak shots are harbingers for the good ones, nothing wasted, the emotion that erupts from inspiration, not in the blink of an eye, but captured in mid-flight. It would be like taking your paintbrush to someone else's canvas. It pisses me off that August isn't more selfish about his art.

"I'm off duty," I say.

I lie back beside him and close my eyes. The sun sits on my eyelids like a warm balloon. I sigh.

August laughs. "You think too much. Go get your camera and we'll go for a walk. See if there's any bricks on the beach."

August collects bricks that wash up from the Otonabee River. There used to be a brickyard in the fifties upriver near the mouth of Katchewanooka Lake. Old water-smoothed bricks get spit out on shore in the spring when the current's stronger. They're unusual colors, yellow and orange, pitted with small bits of white and green glass. August has this little altar in his studio of his best finds, laid out on an old piece of linen on a shelf of planks in his kitchen. I sometimes hear him moving them around at night, the soft clinking of stone on stone. The walls are very thin. I'd much rather listen to him moving his bricks around than the other things I've heard through those walls.

"You don't get out enough," August says. "This is the best season for exploring. Everything's changing."

August covers his eyes with his hand for a second, then brushes his forehead. When he puts his arm back down, his forearm settles on top of mine, heavy, a dead weight. I feel his wrist uncurl, the heel of his hand on the edge of my cuff, his fingers relaxing, coming to rest lightly on the top of my fingers.

"I'm a city girl," I say.

My fingers quiver. I want to slip them between August's fingers and take hold of his hand, stake a claim like some high school signal of romance. Except I can't. August has already been claimed.

"You're scared of the forest aren't you?" he says.

His hand moves off mine.

I open my eyes and sit up. "I am not." August is staring at me.

9

He has blue eyes. Blue Willow China-blue. If he had brown eyes, he'd look fully aboriginal. His history would be exotically veiled behind mysterious earth tone eyes, his culture reflected in that genetic trait. But his features are off-center, like the rest of him is off-center, his eyes as transparent as an ocean, as if he's willing to let you look in because unlike most of us, he has nothing to hide.

"C'mon, let's go," I say. I jump up from the ground and offer a hand to August. He doesn't notice.

"I'm hungry," he says, once he's standing. He pats his stomach with both hands.

"Let's go to The Terminal. Breakfast crowd will be cleared out by now," I say.

August nods. He's easy to please.

The air smells baked with dry leaves, tangy like the inside of a cedar chest.

"You get any good autumn shots?" I say as August bends over to get his camera.

August and I never talk about photography. I've learned his techniques by spying on him in the darkroom. Let's just say August is the real photographer.

"Dunno. I was just taking pictures of the trees," he says.

There's something eerily Norman Rockwell about Watson. It's ninety miles from Toronto, on the eastern edge of cottage country. Most of the sixty thousand people that live here, either work at the Westclock factory, or the new GM plant over in Lakefield. Life moves slowly here. There's a small contained vortex of people under thirty who make little rippling tremors underground, enough to keep things interesting, not too much that they're run out of town. We're talking the quintessential small town. Pickup trucks and baseball hats, cracked sidewalks and big old Victorian houses. They even have a movie theater called The Strand.

As August and I walk over to The Terminal, the streets are empty and silent.

The diner is on King Street down by the Greyhound Bus Terminal. I eat there every day, sometimes breakfast, lunch and dinner. It's the social center of the artistic community in Watson.

It's strange that in a town of sixty thousand there could be an artistic community that not only thrives, but exists unto itself, immune to the influence of Toronto or Ottawa. There are two galleries, a community playhouse, and four bars.

The Terminal Diner, which is like something out of the fifties with its open kitchen and Formica surfaces, has a rotating exhibit of art on the walls along with the placards advertising the daily specials. This month there is a series of black and white paintings done by my favorite waitress, Mia.

Sometimes it feels like everything I need is here, inches from my fingertips.

When we pass the Catholic Church on Simcoe Street, a swarm of little girls come running down the steps, a blur of white in their communion dresses. August and I stop to watch. Their high-pitched voices echo in the air. Mothers shout warnings not to get dirty. I think about August making snow angels in the dirt.

And then I imagine him in a white suit, running after the swarm of little communion girls, swallowed into the middle of their mob as they race down Simcoe Street, his black hair fluttering behind him, an overgrown angel child towering above the rest.

A click beside me breaks the fantasy.

"A gaggle of geese," August says, lowering his camera.

"What?" I exclaim, thinking he's taken a picture of the swarm of little girls.

August doesn't photograph people. He only takes pictures of things. He freelances for the Watson Examiner, and he'll cover fires, accidents, whatever. He just doesn't have any people in his shots. I only photograph people. Things don't come alive under my lens the way they do for August.

"Geese," August repeats, and I see he's pointing to the sky.

A long black V of Canada Geese are honking southward, their mournful cries lost in the shrill squeals of the little communion girls.

"Now I'm really hungry," August says, shaking his head as the geese fly out of sight.

After breakfast, August and I walk back to The Factory and I get my camera. We go to the park and sit on a bench under a weeping willow. We people-watch, our feet stretched out on the patch of dirt under the bench, the crisp smell of burning leaves from someone's backyard hanging in the air.

The grass is still green, but dry yellow leaves flutter across the park as evidence that winter is coming. The trees have bare patches, exposing their fragile brown branches that will rattle like bones when the arctic winds of December come. A dog barks behind us, down by the river. The silence immediately afterwards is a huge hole of melancholy.

"What are you going to bring to the Turkey Fest?" August says, his head turned in the direction of the dog bark.

"Turkey salad?"

Every Thanksgiving Christian has a big party. Everyone has to bring something made with turkey. He used to have the party on American Thanksgiving in November to coincide with the football playoffs, but he got terribly insulted when the party started being referred to as the "Turkey Bowl". So he changed it to Canadian Thanksgiving and now everyone watches hockey.

Last year I moved in a week before the party. I helped Christian decorate his studio with crepe paper turkeys and pumpkins. I made an excuse not to go to the party later and spent the night in my studio listening to the music and laughter across the hall. I was punishing myself. It was stupid.

"I was thinking of making turkey tarts," August says. "We can have them for dessert."

"Original choice," I say. "I'll help you if you like."

August smiles. "Thanks, but Caroline is going to help me. She knows how to make piecrust from scratch."

"Oh," I say.

Caroline is August's girlfriend.

She is a caterer.

"Wendy says Brin's going to come as a turkey," August says.

"Hope nobody sticks a fork in him," I say.

"Christian should make it a costume party," August says. "It's near Halloween. Julie could help us with costumes. I'd like to go as a pilgrim. I've always wanted to wear one of those hats."

I look at August. Either he fails to see the irony of him going as a pilgrim or he's being sarcastic. I can't tell.

"It's cold," I say, and then I shiver as if my words have the power of suggestion.

"Move closer," August says.

When I don't move, he puts his arm around my shoulder and pulls me against him. He relaxes his arm, but it stays across my shoulders.

I want to curl into his chest. I want to slip my hand inside his coat and feel his warmth.

August grips my shoulder and shakes me. "Relax," he says.

"I am relaxed," I say.

"I know what's bugging you," he says.

I stare across the park to George Street, letting the pause grow long enough that I don't have to answer.

"You're homesick aren't you?" he says. "The holiday coming up and... I guess Vancouver is a long way to go for Thanksgiving."

After working so hard to be impenetrable, sadness flows to the surface in a heartbeat. My eyes fill up and I'm teetering on the edge of losing it.

"Anne?"

I nod quickly. August grips my shoulder and pulls me closer. I swallow and swallow, working a smile that won't come, panic rising that I can't talk or I will cry.

August touches my face and his hand accidentally brushes my mouth. It startles me and my head jerks up.

"Sad mouth," he says, quietly.

I work the smile hard and it pops into place. "Is that better?" I say, and then I'm embarrassed by my sarcasm.

August looks away. His arm releases me. A few beats later, he moves his arm from my shoulder and rubs his palms on his jeans.

"Sorry," he says. "It's none of my business where your sadness comes from." He stands up and puts his hands in his pockets. "Just don't…" His shoulders hunch. "Don't stop looking for your joy."

He looks at the ground for a moment, then he turns abruptly and walks away.

I sit on the bench and watch him till he reaches the street. The leaves and grass grow blurry and I let the sadness come. I count to ten. Then I push it away.

August unnerved me. I've seen him do it to other people, disarm them with his simple kindness.

When his hand touched my mouth it felt like a kiss. This weakness is dangerous. August has found a loose string. If I'm not careful, he's going to grab it and pull, and all the seams will rip open and spill my secrets.

Move past it. Quickly.

CHAPTER THREE

The House Of Cards

I've never questioned why I became a photographer. Then again, I've never done what was expected of me. My mother's Methodist upbringing says it is arrogant to want to be extraordinary. Humility is its own reward.

I was arrogant. I wanted the extraordinary. I have been humbled.

Today I'm feeling anxiously humbled. I have to photograph August's girlfriend, Caroline, for a brochure she's doing for her catering company.

Five minutes before she's supposed to arrive, I'm cleaning up my kitchen and trying to get into professional mode. I can't stop thinking about her ability to make piecrust from scratch. It was the way August said it, like she was a deity, able to create something out of nothing.

There's a knock on the door just as I finish putting water in the coffeemaker. Before I can get there, the door opens and Caroline walks in. She's holding a dry cleaning bag over her arm and has a butter-colored leather briefcase in her other hand.

"Good, you're here," she says, walking over to the kitchen table, taking her coat off. She puts the briefcase on the table on top of some contact sheets, then folds the coat and the dry cleaning bag over the back of a chair. "I'm running a little late today. Have to pick up a cake in Ennismore at three. You ready for me?"

"Just about. You want some coffee?"

"Is it perked or brewed?" she says, bracing her arms on the back of the chair.

"It's coffeemaker."

"You really should get a percolator. You can order them from Williams Sonoma. You'd notice the difference."

"Hmm, well... I'm afraid it's coffeemaker coffee today."

Caroline smiles. Her eyes make a quick arc across the room, taking everything in. She's never been in my studio before. "I'll have half a cup," she says.

"Why don't you sit on the stool over by the window," I say. "You want anything in your coffee?"

"Cream," she says over her shoulder.

"Milk?" I say, holding up the carton to show her that's all there is.

I see her inhale and hold a breath. "Fine," she says on the exhale.

Caroline Secord models herself after her hero, Martha Stewart. She went to cooking school in Paris. Probably could have worked as a chef in any restaurant in the world. But she came back to Watson, the town where she was born, and started her own catering company. At twenty-eight, she now has four employees.

Caroline comes from money. Her parents live in Roxton Hill on a ten-acre estate known as Summerhill.

She is blond and beautiful and reminds me of the actress, Rebecca DeMornay, an unabashed sexuality in the way she moves. Her mouth is sensuous, her voice sultry, her eyes blue-green like a storm coming. She is confident, comfortable in her own skin, and loves her German shepherd, Maxine, more than anything.

August met her five years ago when they were newly minted adults of twenty-three. Maxine was tied to a parking meter in front of the grocery store. The parking meter was snapped in two by a car driven by an eighty-four year old woman. Maxine's front leg was run over and her leash got caught under the car's bumper. August was photographing the post office across the street and ran over to stop the woman as she prepared to drive off and drag Maxine with her. August carried Maxine ten blocks to the vet, her blood soaking his shirt, Caroline running beside, begging him to not let her dog die. Maxine survived and Caroline was impressed enough by August's heroism that she pursued him for six months until he dropped Lilly Crowfeather and started dating her.

Every Friday night, Caroline comes over to August's studio and he cooks for her. Their ritual always starts out the same, the sound of plates and pots, the murmur of voices, some laughter, some music.

After dinner it begins.

I cover my ears, but it gets in anyway.

Why do I put up with this?

What?

This place is filthy. You and your damn bricks. You live like a homeless person.

Sorry.

You're lucky I come here at all. Say it.

I'm lucky.

And you're dirty.

I'm dirty.

Now fuck me. I've had a hard day.

When I see August the next day, I can't reconcile him with the person I heard next door the night before. It was someone else. No one could look that beautiful after being told they're dirty.

"So business is going good?" I say, putting some Tungsten film in my 35mm.

Caroline is pulling the plastic off the dry cleaning bag. She removes a white jacket from the hanger. "Business is excellent. Daddy and I drew up a five-year plan and I've just exceeded my profit projection for the year." She slides her arms into the white jacket, adjusting the fold-up collar, fluffing her hair over her shoulders. "And it's only September," she adds, giving me a wide-eyed smile.

"Wow," I say, wondering what a 'five-year plan' is.

Caroline fastens the cloth toggle buttons on the jacket and I realize it's a chef's coat, not a blazer.

"You have a hat to go with the coat?" I ask.

Caroline looks up from the buttons, her face blank.

"You know – the mushroom things," I say, my hand circling my head.

"God no, those things are so ugly."

"Chef Paul wears one."

Caroline smiles. "My point exactly."

I have Caroline sitting sideways to the window, the natural light on her right side. I use an umbrella light for her left side. Through the viewfinder I like the combination of tones, blues and yellows, which will compliment her blond hair and complexion.

Caroline slides off the stool and goes over to her briefcase. She digs inside and pulls out a wooden spoon that looks like it's never been used, the wood bleached and pristine. She goes back to the stool, slides up on the seat, rolls her shoulders, arranges her hair so it falls over her shoulders, adjusts her slim black skirt, crosses her legs, pointing the toe of her black stiletto pump, then crosses her arms, positioning the spoon so it's sticking out of the crook of her arm. She tosses her head once more, then says, "Okay, I'm ready."

It's a pretty good pose. She looks very professional, serious, like she's ready to beat some egg whites till they surrender.

"Do you want some full body as well as head and shoulders?" I say.

Caroline looks directly into the camera. "I think full body would be better," she says, shifting sideways, exposing more of her bare legs.

I make some adjustments and snap a test shot.

Caroline twitches at the sound of the shutter. "I wasn't ready," she says.

"I'm just doing some warm-up shots."

"I only need one good one," she says.

When I look again, her pose has changed. Her face and limbs look stiff. I snap a few more shots, hoping she'll get used to the sound of the shutter and relax. After three, I see that's not working.

"So how's Maxine?" I ask to distract her. "Still chasing raccoons?"

At the mention of Maxine, her eyes open to the light.

"She nearly caught one the other day," Caroline says, swinging her foot. "She tried to climb the maple behind my office. I had to call Suzanne, my assistant, to get the hose." The heel of her pump pops loose. "For the raccoon, not Maxie. She *hates* water. Bath time is *not* her favorite activity." Everything's in motion now, the swinging foot, the flapping shoe, the wooden spoon keeping time.

I start snapping shots randomly. Caroline's animation is wonderful, adding a layer of whimsy on top of her sensuality. My heart picks up, waiting for the moment I will see it, the one perfect shot.

Getting people to talk about themselves forces their personality to the surface. Sometimes I feel like a perfumer, extracting their essence. The trick is to get them to stop thinking, to catch them before they start posing. It's harder than you think. Some people have refined their public face so well, they're incapable of showing a natural angle.

Caroline runs out of Maxine-isms shortly and in the silence that falls, the shutter click sounds louder than normal. I'm not there yet and Caroline's public face resurfaces. It's too blunt, her stare a little too intimidating, the wooden spoon clutched too tightly in her hand.

"Have you got enough pictures yet?" she asks, twisting her neck like it's stiff.

"I want to give you a variety to choose from," I say. I'm wondering if I should put some music on, but I only do that when I'm shooting my art stuff, not with my paying clients. I feel a tingle of doubt starting. I usually don't have a problem with this kind of work.

It's more about pleasing the client, not my own aesthetic. I guess I'm having trouble seeing Caroline without seeing her connection to August. I'm wondering if, despite the fact that August doesn't photograph people, he's ever taken a picture of Caroline.

"Has August ever shot you?"

"Shot me?" Caroline stares at me indignantly. "You mean with a bow and arrow? Because he's Ojibwe?"

My face goes red. "No, no. I meant has he ever photographed you."

She grins. "I'm just funning with you. You should have said 'photographed'."

"Sorry. I figured you'd have heard that expression. You know… 'to shoot someone', 'got some great shots'."

Caroline looks at the clock above my door. "Photography's not really my thing." She examines the wooden spoon, picking some splinters off the handle and flicking them on the floor.

"Except of course for August's stuff," I say.

Caroline sighs and looks up at the ceiling. She squints at something. "You have a really big spider up there," she says. She looks back at me. "August's not that serious about photography. It's more of a hobby with him, until he finds what he really wants to do with his life."

"Wow," I say, looking into the viewfinder to hide my shock.

"You sound surprised," Caroline says.

"Well, it's just that he's really good."

"Compared to who?" Caroline says, tilting her head.

I snap a picture to capture her expression. I look up over the camera. "Compared to just about every photographer I know."

"Does that include yourself?" Caroline says, smiling as if she expects me to deny it.

"Definitely myself included. I'm an amateur compared to him. His eye is so developed. God, his nature shots are gorgeous. So artful. It amazes me how he can narrow his focus and pick the perfect shot. And his sense of composition is brilliant. It's like he sees something human in his subjects even though they're not human." I realize I'm gushing and look at Caroline.

She's staring at me with interest. "You seem to have thought about this a lot."

I look in the camera and out of the corner of my eye I see the edges of the camera's body, nearly as wide as my face, almost, not quite.

I finally get the shot without trying. The best shot is relaxed and playful, sexy and strong. Caroline becomes more confident. She tries different poses without my prompting, twisting sideways as a sultry chef, sitting with her hands on her knees as a prim chef. She kicks off her shoes and poses with one bare foot extended. I'd hire her to cater a party if I saw that photograph.

"So I'll need the pictures by Thursday," Caroline says when we're done.

It's Tuesday and I have another job to print for tomorrow.

When I hesitate Caroline asks, "Is that going to be a problem?"

"No. No problem. How 'bout I get a contact sheet to you tonight and you can select the ones you want printed by tomorrow."

She pulls the plastic dry cleaning bag back over the chef's jacket. "That would be super." She puts her coat on and picks up her brief-case. "You're a doll to do this for me. Thanks again."

"No problem. Should I drop the contact sheet at your office?"

"Oh if you could, that would be wonderful. If it's not too much trouble."

"No, I'd be happy to."

Caroline smiles and it transforms her face. She's very beautiful when she smiles.

"You really should be doing this for a living, Anne," she says.

I laugh.

She looks at me for a moment, then waves goodbye and rushes out the door.

I'm up till three a.m. developing and printing the contact sheets. There are several good shots, which I mark for Caroline. When I'm done, I run over to her office on George Street and drop them in her mailbox. The autumn wind is warm and blows through my hair as I walk back to The Factory, the streetlights pulling me in and out of the shadows. I sleep for a few hours, then get up to finish my other job.

Caroline leaves the contact sheet under my door while I'm taking a nap the next afternoon. She only marked one alternative choice other than the ones I suggested. I get up and print them out, working till three a.m. again. I put the prints and my invoice in an envelope and run them down to her office, go home and sleep till the next evening.

When I come back from dinner that night, I find a cheesecake sitting in front of my door, the box tied with a beautiful brown satin ribbon and sealed with a gold sticker from Caroline's company. There's a card with the box.

> It was a joy having you take my picture.
> The cheesecake is a token of my gratitude.
>
> Thanx, Caroline

I'm surprised by her generosity. The cheesecake is so good, I eat half of it in one sitting. I finish it off the next afternoon.

A week later, I'm still waiting for my invoice to be paid. I call Caroline's office and get her assistant, Suzanne.

"I don't know about any invoice," she says, "But I know we delivered a cake to your address."

It dawns on me a day later. I've been paid in cheesecake.

Covering my tracks seemed easy when I first moved to Watson. Just don't leave a paper trail. I pay for everything in cash and have everyone pay me in cash. I liked the simplicity of it initially, free from the seductive hell of credit cards, and the waste of ink and trees writing checks. Thankfully no one has asked for my social insurance number. I get very little mail other than my phone bill (deposit paid in cash, monthly charges paid in cash). I don't have a bank account in Watson, though when I'm really stuck I dip into my old account in Toronto. Watson has little in the way of shopping, so I haven't bought any clothes or useless stuff for my studio. I've been one step away from the back to basics economics of the barter system. I just didn't think it would come to that.

Without my name on anything, my identity is slowly being erased. I'm beginning to see the appeal of nametags and tattoos.

I knock on Christian's door, a wad of bills in my hand. Waiting for him to answer, I look at a twenty-dollar bill, running my finger over the rough fleshy texture of the paper. The Queen's face stares up at me, benevolent, stoic, trustworthy. Someone has drawn a mustache on her. I turn the bill over. The loon swimming on a lake has a cartoon bubble coming out of its mouth, and in it, it says, MONEY IS ANARCHY.

The door opens. Christian runs a hand through his hair and yawns. "Is it time for breakfast already?" he says.

"It's Saturday. Just came to give you my rent."

Christian looks at the money in my hand. "When are you going to join the human race and get a bank account like a normal person?" he says.

"Don't trust banks," I say. I always say the same thing.

Christian shakes his head and takes the money. "What happens if I get robbed before I get to the bank?"

"Yeah, right. Who'd be dumb enough to rob you?"

Christian motions with his head for me to come in. "Fine. Make me some coffee."

"Sorry, gotta do some prints," I say, avoiding his eyes. He smells like delicious sleep.

"Miss Hanes, you're mean and cruel," he says.

"I just gave you two hundred bucks."

"Next time write me a check and make me some coffee."

I wave to him over my shoulder, cross the hall and go into my studio. I didn't have to look him in the eyes once.

Truth is, I'm embarrassed.

I had a dream about Christian last night.

Let me first describe Christian. He's tall, about six-two, thick blond ponytail, face of a Nordic God. Hazel eyes, ringed with green, always looking for something beyond the surface. He's tanned and healthy, like a ski instructor, has big powerful hands, but he's gentle. He has a radio voice. Talks a lot. I like to listen. I could listen to him for hours. He's funny, smart, gregarious, somewhat opinionated, but charming in his earnest appeal that everyone agree with him. He wears those hip thermal, lumberjack clothes. Let's just say in Toronto, women would be stabbing each other with forks to get to the head of the line.

I have thought about it before, me and Christian. But there's a barrier there. I'm attracted to him, but all from a safe distance, like I'm admiring him through the lens of my camera.

I've told him too many lies.

No, it's more than that. He was the first person I lied to. He was the first person that heard me say, "I'm Anne Hanes." Don't know. It just got easier after that. The first lie is always the hardest.

I met Christian last year in the beer store one Friday night, before I'd moved here. I was staying with a friend in Bobcaygeon, trying to decide what to do with my life, trying to decide if I was a pornographer or not. I'd gone into Watson that day to buy underwear and ended up with a job after seeing an ad in Eaton's for a photographer to take wallet photos. I was low on cash. Seemed safe enough even for me. I *am* a photographer and any risk of me demonizing pictures of little kids with toy train props disappeared when I gave them a fake name.

Christian clicks with people and we clicked that day. We kept running into each other when I started commuting to town for my job, and the life stories were pending. I made one up because the truth was too scary. I told him I was from Vancouver and that I was trying to get out of this bad relationship with my boyfriend in Bobcaygeon. You can lie with ease when you don't think it'll matter. By the time I realized I'd made a friend, it was too late to back out. Truth is, I felt encouraged to lie, blessed in my lie, because at that point I was so used to people in Toronto either spitting on me or giving me the sympathetic head tilt like I had some incurable disease, I was greedy for the unconditional acceptance Christian, and then everyone else in Watson gave me for not being who I really was. Christian told me about the vacant studio at The Factory and at the time I reasoned that I'd already painted the picture so I might as well jump into it. Typical reckless move.

There's always been more guilt in my friendship with Christian because he witnessed the birth of my phony life. By the time I met everyone else here, I was already Anne Hanes, like I'd auditioned for the role, got the part and was already in character.

I know a shrink would tell me the reason I dreamt about Christian is that he is the one person I have the most to hide from. So of course I would dream I was naked.

We were making love in a sauna. And the sauna was in the middle of the forest. A little wood shack surrounded by those creepy pines. The residue of the dream is all mood and shapes, white flesh and green trees, blond wood and blond hair, steam and black sky, sweat and chill night air.

He was so unapologetically carnal. We were like Adam and Eve. Dreams are bullshit.

The next morning when I look in the mirror and say my name, it sounds odd. I wait and say it again. Watching my lips move, I have a rush of panic. My face and name don't go together.

I think I'm going to stop doing my morning mirror ritual.

Later that afternoon the sky turns gray and the temperature drops to thirty-five degrees. The wind pushes out of the north, blue-tinged and cold. A half-time show of flurries whips down Water Street caught in the rings of light from the street lamps that have come on prematurely. I turn on the oven to warm my studio and listen to the wood skeleton of The Factory expand and contract in the cold. The world looks lonely outside my window.

I put on my jacket and walk down to The Terminal Diner.

A block down George Street, I see August coming out of Sam The Record Man. He stops and looks up at the sky as a new round of snow flurries starts falling like confetti. He extends the tip of his tongue, then licks his lips and smiles. When he sees me, he turns and spread his arms straight out.

"Lucky sign," he says. "Snow in September."

I walk up to him and he lowers his arms.

"I think it's a sign they should turn the heat on," I say. "My studio's like a barn."

"Ah," August says. "You need a space heater. Where you going?"

"To the diner where I know they have heat and hot coffee. What'd you buy at Sam's?"

August lifts the red plastic bag in his hand. "The new Robbie Robertson and a best of Billie Holiday. You want to listen? I have hot coffee and a space heater."

"Sure," I say, and we fall into step up George Street as the snow swirls and lands like miniature flowers in August's black hair.

"What's snow in September a lucky sign of?" I ask.

August puts Billie Holiday in his CD player and pushes play. His studio is warm, the floor lamps throwing yellow light up the brick walls.

He straightens up, tucking his hair behind one ear. "My grandmother said it was a sign of cleansing. That everyone was about to experience a rebirth, rid themselves of a burden, or walk out of a period of sadness."

"Wow," I say, curling my hands around the hot coffee cup. "I like that. It's so positive."

"My grandmother was optimistic," August says, sitting down at the table across from me. Billie Holiday croons sweet and low in the background.

I like August's studio. It doesn't look temporary. The walls are mottled with white paint, patches of red brick showing through. He's hung large prints of his building photos in old frames he found in junk shops and stripped to their natural wood. Some are ornate, curlicues of carved wood, some simple with beveled edges. The photos are mostly black and white, the Westclock Factory, the post office, the town hall clock tower, The Factory in winter, the window sills trimmed with snow.

He has really cool old furniture. A wine velvet couch with carved wood arms, a claw foot coffee table, chrome floor lamps with milky glass shades. Behind a folding screen he made from an old factory window panel with bubbled glass, there's a brass bed that's taken on a bronze patina with age. It's covered with an old red quilt, a Hudson Bay blanket folded at the foot.

His large floor to ceiling windows are in the bedroom overlooking Water Street. The windows are hung with long lace curtains that drape on the floor and let in delicate patterns of light from the street lamps.

His kitchen is the only oddity. There's an old wooden table with carved legs and an assortment of mismatched antique chairs, a mirrored sideboard where he keeps his dishes, an eclectic collection of junk store china. The furniture has the richness of many histories. But the kitchen itself looks like it came through the wall from another apartment. The counters are stainless steel, and the sink has an industrial faucet with a hose sprayer. The stove is enormous, a Jenn-Air with six burners, the fridge a modern tower of stainless steel with the freezer on the bottom. August has an expensive-looking coffeemaker that grinds the beans for you, plus an espresso machine I've never seen him use, as well as a percolator.

The first time I saw August's studio, I said he must be really serious about cooking. He said Caroline had the reno done and bought him the appliances for his birthday. "I think she was trying to inspire me to cook more than Kraft Dinner," he said. Then he unlocked the steamer trunk in his utility room and showed me his stash. It was full of Kraft Dinner, Fig Newtons and Captain Crunch. "You don't need to mention this to her," he said. "She thinks I keep my camera equipment in here." I thought it was funny at the time.

August looks into his coffee cup, then dips his finger in and fishes out a coffee ground. "I'm sorry about bringing up Vancouver the other day," he says.

"Vancouv... Oh, that. No problem."

August looks at me for a moment, like he's not sure if I mean it, or I'm just being polite.

"Really. It's okay," I say.

"Are you going to stay?" August says.

I hold up my empty cup. "If you make more coffee."

August looks at the cup in my hand. "I meant are you going to stay in Watson?"

"Why do you ask?" I say.

August looks at the kitchen wall that separates our studios. "I don't know. Your place looks..."

"Temporary?"

"No. I don't know, not lived in. You still keep your clothes in a suitcase."

"I'm a slob," I say, my tongue wrinkling with embarrassment. "And I'm really lazy."

August laughs. "So lazy it takes you a year to unpack?" He gets serious again. "Do you like it here?"

"Yeah," I say. "The work's pretty good. Sometimes pays better than others, but I'm doing okay. And I like the people here."

"You're better than this," August says.

"Better than what?"

"Better than the stuff you get hired for here. Anyone can take class pictures and wallet photos."

"It's a living."

"Is that how you made your living in Vancouver?"

I look away and study August's sideboard. I can see the back of his head reflected in the mirror. "No. Look, I'm happy here. Life's simple."

"You don't strike me as a simple person."

August picks up my coffee cup and gets up from the table.

"Do I look like I'm high maintenance or something?" I say. "'Cause I'm not. You've seen my place. I can't even be bothered to hang my clothes up."

"There's a difference between living simple and not planning things. I'm surprised you moved here. It doesn't look like you meant to. It's more like you wandered into Watson by accident. I'm just wondering if you're planning on staying and if so, why haven't you unpacked your suitcase?"

I watch August's back as he stands at the counter making another pot of coffee. I don't know what compels me to say it, but I ask, "Do you think I should stay?"

August doesn't turn around, but I can tell he's thinking about his answer. "I think you deserve better, but... Yeah, I do."

I can't sleep that night. My lie has penetrated my life too deeply. I have actually pictured my fictional life in Vancouver. I imagined the apartment I lived in, the restaurants I ate in, the kind of car I drove. I've built a house of cards.

Rolling over in bed, I see my open suitcase, shoes scattered around it, shirts draped over the open top. I get out of bed and open the closet by the front door. The metal hangers ping against each other and an empty musty smell rises up into my face. I gather up all my clothes and drop them in a heap in front of the closet. Then I hang them up, one by one.

When I get back into bed, my heart is beating fast. I'm not sure what I've just committed to.

When I wake up after three hours of sleep, I go to the mirror, dazed and confused, and say the wrong name. There's a brief moment after I say, "Anne Hanes" where my voice and my reflection align. Then I realize my mistake and my little inner voice tries to let me off the hook. *It's okay. Why not just let yourself be Anne. What's the harm?* Albertine seems like the fantasy, like my fictional world in Vancouver.

That's when I realize I'm having a serious identity crisis.

Later that day, when I'm shooting Mia in my studio, I realize my photography is also suffering an identity crisis.

Lately, I've been shooting indoors using as much natural light as possible. Mother Nature invented light and shadow. I've been letting her control the mood of my shoots. Rainy days, gray skies, I shoot strong and dark. Bright sunny days, I shoot energetic and carefree.

Today, the light is odd and evasive and so is my mood.

Mia has become my favorite model and I ask her to pose for me whenever she has some free time from the diner.

She has been a waitress at The Terminal Diner since she was sixteen. She's nineteen now. She calls herself "an artist-in-training". She paints. Christian lets her use his studio since she still lives at home. She leads a double life. If you ask her what she does, she'll say she's a waitress, but when you see her paintings, you know that's what's in her heart.

She left school to help support her family. Her father painted the fluorescent numbers on alarm clocks at the Westclock factory for years until he started having health problems. They moved him to the assembly line with Mia's mother where they put the finished clocks in boxes. Sometimes he can't work. He gets headaches, his joints swell. No one knows exactly what's wrong with him.

Mia paints in black and white. Not one speck of color. She paints pictures of houses and buildings, realistic reproductions in exact detail, like black and white photographs. She dresses in black and white too, doesn't own one piece of colored clothing. Her only deviation is to wear gray. When she works at the diner, she looks like an angel in her white uniform, white stockings and white shoes. I was convinced for the longest time she was color blind and playing it safe.

I met her at Christian's a week after I moved into The Factory. She was working on an enormous canvas of the Westclock factory that was incredible. I told her so. Her smile cemented our friendship. Mia's like that. She drifts towards people like a small ship and docks beside you.

She's very easy to photograph. I shot a lot of professional models in Toronto who had so much attitude, so conscious of their beauty it was nearly impossible to catch them out of pose. I referred to them as 'little hair-flipping goddesses". When I was shooting for myself, I picked unprofessional models. I liked using dancers for their unrefined beauty. They may not have beautiful faces, but their bodies have an odd perfection. They have a natural grace that makes them look relaxed even in awkward poses. Their personality is in the way they move, and I learned the hard way that there is mystery in their silence.

Mia has that grace. She has a dancer's body, long legs, long torso, long slender arms. Her feet are incredible, like a Rodin sculpture, lots of tendon and bone. She has an unusual face, a straight razor thin nose, a pointed chin, but very full bee-stung lips. Her eyes are large, brown, so dark they look black. Her hair is a force of nature, like some lush overgrown bush, reddish brown corkscrew curls that trail down her back to her waist. When she's working, she braids it in a long thick ponytail. The color of her skin is what makes her fascinating to photograph. She's pale, not white, but ivory, like wedding satin. It's as if she is illuminated from within, projecting light instead of reflecting it. I like to shoot her in black and white to catch all the

31

gradations of gray.

Today I am shooting Mia in front of the window on a portable set of stairs I borrowed from Christian. I have some Satie on the CD player, melancholy music, not too rhythmic or my model will start moving unconsciously. If I wanted movement I'd put on Professor Longhair.

Mia arches over the top stair, head thrown back. The light comes in over the top of her body. There is a stark shadow under her chin, throat and sternum. Her collarbones are stretching out of her skin. I think of dinosaur bones. I get an idea. Maybe I should try shooting Mia outside with one of Christian's sculptures.

I feel a surge of ambition. It's been a long time. Then I remember.

I've been having this problem with my finger. It's been happening off and on for the last two months. My finger is on the shutter button and it freezes. I see the image through my lens, my eye frames it, I know what it will look like printed already and then... I hesitate. My mind starts spinning and I'm trying to hang on to my thoughts long enough to process them and at the same time, I don't want to process them. What am I committing to? Is this shot okay? Will people like it? Will they judge it? Is there anything wrong with it? Then I start breaking it down. What's in the background? What does their expression say?

Strange that this problem is selective and only affects me when I'm shooting for myself. My paying work, portrait sittings, class pictures, all come easy, as if someone else lined up the shot, posed the bodies, told them to smile, then all I had to do was step in and click.

When I was shooting Caroline the previous week, I felt it stirring under the surface, the tickle of doubt trying to rise. I managed to control it.

Mia is getting restless in front of the camera.

"You want me to try something else?" she says, shifting her arms.

The piano music is plinking in the background. The light is constant and pale from the window, as unwavering as a stare.

I can't answer. Maybe she should. Maybe this is the right shot. I don't know.

My finger moves from the focus to the shutter button. Automatic. Then the wave of hesitation hits me. Mia is frozen in her pose. There's a buzzing in my ears, like a swarm of angry insects. Indecision. Then fear. Then more fear about my indecision. I wait, my finger hovering, pressing the button halfway, feeling the give, testing the motion, unable to commit to pressing it down all the way.

"Hurry, or I'm gonna be like this permanently," Mia says, her voice strained in her throat from trying to hold her head back.

I can't move.

I've shrunk from the scene, my whole being fixated on what I see out of one eye. My body isn't there anymore. I'm floating behind the camera, no arms, no legs.

The piano plinks the ending of one piece. There's a moment of silence between tracks on the CD.

I hear a noise behind me, a door opening, though it sounds like it's in the distance. When I hear footsteps, I realize it's closer. A floorboard shifts under my feet.

My eye is jammed in the viewfinder, the rim of the socket cold against my cheekbone.

I feel someone behind me.

My finger hovers over the shutter button, then back on. I lick my lips, draw in a breath and hold it, like I'm about to duck my head under water.

I feel someone at my back, a piece of clothing brushing my shirt, heat from the body underneath, and then the impression of a shoulder leaning into me, a row of ribs pressing against my side.

I wait.

My finger touches the shutter button again, then moves off.

I feel a rush of air past my ear, an arm raised beside mine, the heat of an open palm a split second before I feel the touch of skin over my hand on the shutter button.

Fingers grasp mine, a little pressure, enough of a squeeze to gently guide my finger back on the button. I feel the index finger curl over mine, the breath in my ear, holding, like I'm holding.

The finger presses my finger down.

The shutter clicks.

I close my eye the second it happens so I don't even see the picture committed.

I let out my breath and turn around. My hand is still curled in his hand.

"Don't think," August says, easing my fingers out one by one.

I'm numb like a junkie after the rush has passed, staring up into August's face, letting him stroke my fingers. Then he curls my fingers into my palm and lets go of my hand, stepping back, looking at Mia and smiling.

He brushes his hand across the top of his head and let's out a breath. "Hey, Mia. How's it going?"

Mia is leaning back on her hands, her eyes going from me to August, then back to me. I look away.

"Okay," she says and smiles her shy smile. She gets up, jumps off the stairs and walks over to August.

My chest feels full and I'm a little nauseous.

"Can I have a beer?" Mia asks me.

"I don't have any." I don't mean to say it so bluntly.

Mia looks at me for a moment, then says, "I'll go see if Christian does." She waits another moment, as if she expects me to say something else.

August is standing with his hands in his back pockets looking out the window, his eyes squinting at something in the distance.

"I'll see you guys later," Mia says. She touches August's arm.

He nods and goes back to looking out the window.

"Thanks," I mumble.

Mia slips out the door, closing it quietly behind her.

As soon as she's gone, August pivots on his heel and looks at me.

I take my time getting the film out of my camera. I can't believe I let him witness my hesitating finger.

"You want me to develop those for you?" August says.

He's never offered to develop photographs for me before. I study the roll in my hand.

"Sure." I hand him the film.

"I'll be in the darkroom," he says.

"Okay," I say, unscrewing my camera from the tripod.

August walks to the door, opens it and stops. "You can't wait for the moment to happen," he says.

I look up.

He has his eyes closed, like he's trying to find some elusive words. "You're not taking her picture. She's allowing you to have that moment. You just have to let it happen." He opens his eyes. Their blueness startles me. "Forget about every photograph you've taken. You'll miss the next one that's waiting to be taken."

He nods once, opens the door and walks out, bouncing my roll of film up and down in his hand.

Later on I walk down the hall to the darkroom. The red light above the door is off. I hear water running inside.

I knock on the door. "August?"

"Enter at your own risk," he answers.

For half an hour I watch him work. His approach is so intuitive he doesn't time anything. He seems to know by instinct when to take the paper out of the bath, as if it's his magic that makes the photograph develop and not the chemicals.

August pulls the photograph of Mia out of the final bath and I'm surprised it turned out so well.

"You're really good at this," I say.

August hangs the photograph up. "I didn't take it. You did."

"I kind of feel like we both took it."

August is looking at the picture. "I just helped. Probably shouldn't have. It looked like you were having trouble."

"Yeah, you're right. Sometimes I think too much."

August turns and looks at me. "But the moment wasn't going to get any better."

"I wasn't sure it was the right moment." I see a bit of impatience in August's eyes. "Well how do you know when it's the right moment?" I ask.

"You see them going by. They're all good, you just have to capture one." He lifts his hand and snatches the air.

"Is that what you do?"

August turns away from me and lifts the corner of one of the prints, leaning in to look at it. "Sort of. I like to stop time."

"You mean like preserving the past?"

He keeps looking at the print, a shot of Mia I did the week before. "No, like holding back the future."

Neither of us says anything for a moment. I want him to say more. He's never talked this much about photography with me.

"But if you're not preserving the past," I say, "which I thought was the role of a photographer, and you're refusing the future, then aren't you just living in the present? Which is sort of like having amnesia and denying yourself the right to dream."

August turns around. "Photography isn't about something that's already happened. It's taking an event and keeping it in the present. Stopping time. Keeping the moment alive."

I think of the vitality in August's photographs, the way the trees still seem to be moving.

"I guess I've never seen the pictures as events. I think of them as documentations of a personality. But then people are all I photograph."

"People are hard," August says, watching me. "They don't always show what's underneath."

"That's true. A tree is a tree. A building, a building. Maybe I should change my subject matter."

"No, you're good at doing people. It's hard to have that kind of objectivity."

"Yeah, well, sometimes I'm not that objective. I over think it and start doubting my ability, and sometimes I'm not critical enough and do stuff that shouldn't be seen by anyone and afterwards I seriously doubt my…" I stop. I've said way too much.

August moves closer. "Doubt your what?"

He holds my eyes and I feel the words being pulled out of me. "My judgement."

That was a scary confession, a little too close to the truth, but the way August is looking at me makes me want to confess more.

The air seems to buzz, the hum of the overhead fan like a song playing far away, a good song, the kind that makes your heart trip. August is motionless, but his stillness is only on the surface. It's one of those electric moments when you know something is about to happen. He raises his arm and reaches towards my cheek.

There's a knock on the door.

A muffled female voice calls from the other side. "August?"

A wave of heat races up my neck into my face.

August drops his arm and steps away from me.

The doorknob rattles, then the door opens and a column of light floods the room. August and I are blinking like moles.

Caroline steps into the room and stops, her head turning to August, then to me, then back to August.

"I was just helping Anne do some prints," August says.

"Oh, can I see?" Caroline says, walking further into the room.

August looks surprised, but only for a second. He steps aside and motions Caroline over to the clothesline where my prints are drying.

"Oh, it's Mia!" Caroline says. "She looks so beautiful." She's looking at the shot that August helped me take.

Caroline turns to me. "Like I said, Anne, you really should be doing this for a living."

August releases a sigh, then a tense laugh. "She does do this for a living."

CHAPTER FOUR

Into the Scary Pines

My father was an inventor, an electronics whiz. He designed sophisticated alarm systems for factories, measuring devices, and different kinds of meters. He died on the golf course. My father wasn't a golfer. He'd developed a meter to measure water absorption in the ground and was out there one Sunday at the eighteenth hole, inserting his device, a four-foot tube of steel, into the ground. The tube acted like a lightning rod. My father got zapped while holding his invention in his arms. The bolt of lightning blew his shoes off. They never found the left one.

My brother, Aaron, said my father was a hopeless optimist waiting for his epiphany. He was pragmatic when it came to raising his family, but down in his basement workshop he was a mad scientist given to giddy moments of inspiration. He'd often wake in the middle of the night and go down to the kitchen to write down an idea that had come to him in a dream; the burglar alarm that talked to you, the telephone that printed out the daily newspaper (long before the invention of the fax machine), a laser that closed surgical incisions. If he'd lived longer, he would have seen the progress in technology that would have made his dreams possible. I feel like he's missed out on all the fun. He would have loved the Internet.

Unfortunately, his epiphany was delivered in the form of a lightning bolt and he probably had time for one more flash of foresight: never stand on a golf course in a lightning storm holding onto a steel tube.

My mother took his death stoically. In the first few months she wore an expression of surprise. One day it was gone, replaced by a chin-thrust-forward determination, the kind of look she used to get when I was a kid and she was about to tackle stripping and waxing the floors. The rest of us had buried our grief so deep, we acted as if nothing had happened. We didn't talk about him. Aaron left for good. Arvo, Angela and I talked around his death as though a criminal act had been committed and we were embarrassed.

I became an adult when my father died. Childhood ends the moment you witness mortality. My father illustrated death for me far more than my grandfather did. Grampa died of old age after living a full life. My father's full potential was never realized.

He died nine years ago, when I was twenty. Sometimes I still think about him in the present and it hits me. He's gone. I can't talk to him anymore. The grief sneaks up on me so suddenly, I have to walk away from it. I can't walk away from my mother.

My relationship with my mother is sometimes an effort. It's a complex arrangement of defenses and stifled honesty. She looks for cracks in my armor, then she gets out her crowbar. I have this uncontrolled reflex. I'm like a swinging door around her, fearfully ajar, ready to slam shut at the slightest movement.

Thankfully, she doesn't call me often. I'm not sure if it's because she's still ticked off that I don't want to be Albertine anymore or if she's respecting my privacy. She's cagey that way, never saying one way or the other, but she sighs a lot whenever I talk to her. When I first told her I'd changed my name, she pretended she found it amusing, like I was playing a childhood game with an imaginary friend. Guess we've passed the point of it being amusing. At least she hasn't repeated that mantra from when I was five; *don't be afraid to be yourself*. Never really understood that phrase until a year ago.

And yet I miss her. When my life fell apart last year, she picked me up and brushed me off, never once showing her disappointment. Sometimes I want to run back to Toronto and tell her I'm sorry. Make it right with her. Not that she acts like I owe her anything, but I feel guilty how badly I fucked things up. Sometimes I feel like she's waiting me out, like I'm just going through a phase she has to endure, then I will come to my senses and reclaim my life. Her optimism drives me crazy.

As for the rest of my family, well, my older sister, Angela, wrote me off immediately. She hasn't spoken to me in over a year. My younger brother, Arvo, occupies a different planet than me. I think he sent me a Christmas card two years ago. My older brother, Aaron, has been wandering from job to job for ten years. I don't even know where he is. I'd like to think he'd understand the choices I've made. We were once kindred spirits.

What is it about families? Despite everything, I cannot deny my connection to these people.

Friends are made by choice, but the memories you share with your family are written in blood. It's a permanent stain.

After the scene in the darkroom with August and Caroline, I feel like I've made a narrow escape from an impending complication. August and I are treading the line of something and I think it would be smart for me to avoid him for a while.

That night, I go out with Christian to The Underdog, a small bar underneath the Red Dog Tavern on Hunter Street. It's the local hangout for the arts community in Watson and the college crowd from Trent University.

Watson only has a few bars. The Roxy on George Street is big, dark, has heavy metal bands. The bikers prefer it 'cause after it closes they can go to the Chinese restaurant next door and hang some more and maybe intimidate a few college kids who've wandered over from The Underdog. Gracie's on Water Street is sedate, dinner and folk music.

The Underdog has a resident band that plays every weekend. The Black Dogs. Wendy's boyfriend, Brin, plays guitar in the band. Their songs are like some kind of indigenous music, with lyrics about larger than life characters in Watson, like Preacher Bill, who went to jail for putting up posters for his band on telephone poles around town. The Black Dogs' song about sled dogs in Bobcaygeon is their anthem. It's always the last song of the evening. Everyone knows the words and sings along and usually someone from the audience jumps up on stage during the third verse and sings with the band.

I'm at The Underdog tonight because I need the therapy of belonging to a clan.

I drink too much and dance under the blue lights in front of the stage, swaying the restlessness out of my body. I keep replaying what August said about wanting to stop time. I'd love to be able to freeze myself in this moment, safe in the crush of bodies around me, with no ties to the past or the future.

I dance till I'm sweating, letting the drums beat in my head to stop me from thinking.

When the band takes a break, I stagger over to the bar. Mia's there, trying to get the bartender's attention.

"Joe. Joe. Joe," she shouts over the canned music and loud voices.

Joe is sailing from one end of the bar to the other like a duck in a carnival shooting gallery. He is one of the larger than life characters in Watson. He once ran for mayor and boasted that his entire campaign cost him fifty cents. It was the price of a cup of coffee that he bought for the woman running against him. She's now the mayor.

"Mia," I yell, sliding up next to her.

She turns and looks at me. There's caution in her eyes.

"I owe you a beer," I say.

"That's okay," she says, turning to lean on the bar, trying to get Joe's attention again.

"No, really," I say. "I was in a bad mood this afternoon. Lemme buy you a beer."

Mia looks down at her folded hands on the bar.

"Please, Mia."

"Why were you in a bad mood?" she says, turning to me.

I stop and think. I'm having trouble focusing on her angelic face. "'Cause you're so beautiful I don't deserve to take your picture," I say, swaying.

Mia starts to smile. Then she moves towards me and before I can refocus on her, she's hugging me. "You're drunk," she says in my ear. "But thanks for saying I'm beautiful."

"Wow-wee," I say, untangling myself from her arms.

Later, Christian has to drag me up Hunter Street.

"Jesus Christ," Christian says, pulling me by the arm when I try and stop to hug a telephone pole in solidarity with Preacher Bill's pro-postering cause. "You are out-of-control."

"I like being out of control!" I yell, tripping over my feet.

"Hanes on the loose," Christian says to some people standing in the parking lot beside the bar.

"Nice singing, Christian," someone yells back.

Christian had the honor of singing the third verse of Sled Dogs from Bobcaygeon tonight.

"Yeah, nice crooning," I say, as Christian jerks me back at the corner of Hunter and George because the light is red.

Christian has his hand hooked on my elbow, and I swing to face him. He's looking very tall in his cowboy boots tonight. I have to look way up.

"Hey, Christian," I say, squinting at him.

Christian sighs and turns to me. "Yes, dear." The light turns green, and he pulls me by the arm across the street.

"I had a dream about you."

He snorts. I trip and he rights me. I start laughing. My jean jacket is slipping off my shoulder. Christian tries to yank it back on, but I stumble and my arm slips out of the sleeve.

"You were buck naked," I say. I start laughing again, and then I can't stop. It's like an attack. The spasms keep rising in my stomach and up into my mouth. I'm laughing so hard, I'm bent over, walking like a crab as Christian continues to drag me up Hunter Street.

I can sense him starting to smile. "You are *way* over the limit," he says.

"Speed limit!" I yell. "Pull me over. Give me a ticket."

When I yank my arm, I catch Christian by surprise and throw him off balance. I fall sideways and my back hits the brick wall of the bakery. A second later, Christian lands flat up against me, knocking the breath out of me.

His body is a dead weight, his shoulders pinning me, his thighs covering mine. It feels good to be weighted down by a warm body, pinned like a butterfly against the wall, mounted for safekeeping.

I slip my arms around Christian's waist, my head finding the curve of his shoulder and burrowing into the warmth and smell of his clothes.

He straightens me up, but only to hold me more comfortably. His hand cups the back of my head. His other arm circles my waist, pulling me tighter against him.

I sigh.

Everything is quiet.

We stand like that for a few minutes without moving and then I hear voices coming down the street. Two female voices.

Christian and I are still like a statue, and I have the irrational thought that if we don't move, no one will notice us.

The voices get nearer, one laughing, the other murmuring. Their footsteps echo off the buildings.

The voices stop in mid-sentence, and Christian and I put a bit of space between us to look.

Christian doesn't exactly push me out of his arms, but he extracts me with one move, setting me a foot away from him.

They've stopped half a block away. I try to focus on their faces. I can tell they're staring. They resume walking towards us.

"Hey, Christian."

It's Julie. She passes us, her smile at Christian, bland

Her friend I don't know. She glares first at Christian, then at me. I hear the sharp click of her tongue hitting the roof of her mouth.

I close my eyes and slump backwards. The wall catches me.

"Shit," I whisper.

Soberly we disengaged, propriety awakened, an awareness of the unfamiliar becoming familiar without intent. Accidental affection. Stepping over the line into each other's personal space because the censors had temporarily shut down.

When Jezebel wakes up the next morning, it feels like dogs are ripping the flesh off the back of her neck.

I wish I could take a picture right now and stop time. I'm really not up to facing today.

When I sit up and swing my legs over the side of the bed, the ball of pain shifts in my head and bounces off the back of my eyes.

I groan.

Julie is the nicest person I know in Watson. And all the rest are pretty damn nice. Okay, so her and Christian haven't worked out what it is between them, but I know, I know she has a serious crush on him. My skin wrinkles with embarrassment. I can see Christian and I in each other's arms. The picture looks so wrong, our guilty faces, caught in the act.

Why can't I ever think two fucking minutes into the future and see the outcome of my actions?

I crawl out of bed and stumble across the room to the kitchen table.

The brown envelope of pictures is still sitting there. It was tucked in the threshold of my door when Christian deposited me there last night after we walked home in awkward silence.

I don't have to open the envelope. I know what's inside. August gathered up my photographs from the darkroom for me. Shit, I feel careless.

I wish I could put my finger on the button, no hesitating, like I'm pushing a detonation switch and time will blissfully stop.

I'm half dressed when someone bangs on the glass pane in my door. It rattles unbelievably loud.

When I open the door and see who it is, I groan again.

"Come on," Christian says, "Let's go. You need a few aspirins, forty cups of coffee and some nice greasy bacon and eggs to knock that hangover out of your system."

"But it's only eight thirty," I say.

"I know," Christian says, walking in the door, forcing me back into the room. "I have to be at work by ten." When I don't move, he says louder. "Come on, come on. Move it!"

"I'm really not up for this."

"Tough," he says, pushing me in the small of my back with his hand.

Christian and I eat breakfast together every morning at the diner. We usually get there after all the regulars have cleared out. They eat at 7:30. We arrive at 8:30 or 9 and there are a few copies of the day's newspaper left over to read. Christian has to do the crossword puzzle every morning or he thinks his mind will go soft.

When Christian and I walk in and take our usual seats at the counter, I have a moment of panic, like I've forgotten to put on some important piece of clothing and now I'm out in public exposing myself.

Mia is behind the counter, coffee pot in hand.

"Hey, buddies. Pot's fresh," she says pouring Christian a cup while I check my shirt to make sure it's buttoned.

The radio on top of the milk dispenser is on its usual country station, a nick-nick-neer of fiddles as Tammy launches into "Stand By Your Man". *Give him two arms to cling to,* she sings and I picture a monkey with long dangling limbs.

"You coming down with something?" Mia says, pouring coffee in my cup.

"I've got a headache," I say.

"Hah," Christian says into his coffee cup.

"I'll get you some aspirin," Mia says, putting the coffee pot down on the counter.

I swivel around on my stool and lean back against the counter. Christian picks up the paper and snaps it open.

Mr. Sepic – who owns the gas station where none of us go because he has a peephole in the ladies washroom that everyone in town knows about – is sitting in his usual spot, back booth facing the door, staring into space. He's like a permanent fixture, bolted to the floor like the table he's sitting at, collecting dust, staring silently around the clock. I wonder if he's always here, never moves in fact, sits in the dark when they close the diner at night and lock the door behind him. Maybe he sits and wonders why he never has any business at his gas station.

I nod to him and he gives me a sad smile back.

I swivel around again, too fast. The stool is floating underneath me. Behind my eyes, my brain is tilting like it's trying to find the horizon. All the blood is flowing to my feet and gravity has suddenly become a concern.

I lean down and rest my head on the cool edge of the counter. "Oh God," I mumble.

Christian lets go of one edge of the newspaper and pats my back. "There, there," he says.

"Here you go," Mia says putting two Bayer tablets by my coffee cup. Christian lifts his head and clears his throat.

"Ah... Miss Hanes here is going to have another thirty-nine cups of coffee, two fried eggs, two strips of bacon, and toast, heavy on the butter. And I'll have the same."

He lifts the paper in both hands and gives it a shake, snapping the pages flat.

Visualizing all that food does me in. My stomach lurches. I swing off the stool and run for the bathroom. As I'm pushing open the door, I hear Christian say. "Oh and she'll need a few more aspirins and some Eno to wash that down."

By two that afternoon I've thrown up for the last time and begun to think it's more than alcohol polluting my system. I feel toxic with lies and deceptions.

To make matters worse, every time I stuck my head in the toilet I heard my sister Angela's voice speaking over the sound of my retching.

Well, I hate to tell you so, but you deserve it. Can't enjoy the tune without paying the piper. A good purge and maybe you'll get your life in order. Get rid of all that poison.

I actually answered her. "Fuck off and die."

When I was seven and Angela was sixteen, I accidentally altered my identity. My father gave me a tin of smoked herring one morning at breakfast. It was one of his odd and loving gestures. He knew I'd appreciate it more than a doll. The tin of herring was a secret communiqué, a symbol of our pact because I loved herring the same way my father loved herring. No one else in my family liked fish. Arvo once threw up at the table, right in his plate, when my mother made the mistake of serving haddock for dinner.

I carried the tin of herring around with me all day, thinking I would share it with my father when he got home from work. The two of us could sit on the back porch and eat out of the tin with our fingers, happily excluding everyone else.

Arvo followed me around all day trying to yank the tin out of my back pocket.

I punched him in the nose. He kicked me in the knee. That's how we communicated.

"Who wants stinky fish," he yelled, holding his nose. "You'll have fish breath. No one will want to be around you."

He called me "stinky fish" for the rest of the day. I didn't care. I had my herring, which elevated me above his jealous taunts.

Time dragged slowly as I waited for my father to come home. When he finally did, I ran around him in circles waving the tin.

"You haven't eaten it yet?" he said.

"Waiting for you," I said.

"Not now, honey. Where's your mother?" He pushed me aside.

Of course I was always the last to know. My parents were going out for the evening to play bridge at the neighbors. He didn't have time to sit and eat fish with me. I was crushed.

I cried. Angela was informed she was babysitting. I cried harder.

By 8:30 I'd stopped crying, but I was so mad at my father for not wanting to share the herring, I figured I'd eat the whole tin myself.

I examined the tin, which until now, I hadn't contemplated having to open on my own. It was one of those long rectangular tins with a flip-up tab that peeled back the metal top.

I couldn't budge it. I took it to Angela, who was engrossed in *The Mod Squad* on TV.

"Open this."

Angela waved me away. "Get that stinking can of fish out of my face," she yelled.

"But, I want to eat it now," I pleaded.

"Open it yourself then," she said.

I went back in the kitchen and found a screwdriver in my mother's utility drawer. I used it to pry up the metal tab. Arvo watched, fascinated with the potential for disaster with tools.

I managed to pop the lid. I pulled and pulled, straining to peel the metal top back. It finally ripped with the ringing scrape of bending tin. The herring oil splattered down the front of my shirt. An oily glob hit Arvo in the face. He screamed and ran into the living room.

"She got me! She got me!"

"Oh, for Christ's sake," Angela yelled, jumping up from the couch.

I walked smugly into the living room, waving the sharp metal lid over my head.

"Herring," I said, triumphantly.

"Put that down before you cut yourself," Angela said, shoving Arvo away as he tried to wipe his face on her sweater.

"Can't make me," I said, waving the piece of tin at her.

I went back in the kitchen, but now I was curious. The metal top didn't look that sharp. I tested with my thumb.

First there was just a long vertical dent in my skin. Then there was a lot of blood. My flesh parted, revealing the raw insides of my thumb, which resembled stewing beef.

"Ahhhh," I screamed running into the living room, my thumb in the air, two red rivers of blood flowing down my wrist.

Arvo's scream made Angela jump from the couch like she'd sat on a pin.

"Jesus Christ!" she screamed. "What the hell did you do?"

Arvo screamed again and ran for the front door. Before Angela could stop him, he was out and across the driveway to the neighbors where my parents were playing bridge.

Angela dragged me by my good arm down the hall to the bathroom. She stuck my bloody hand under the cold faucet. I watched my blood swirl down the drain like wisps of red smoke.

"I told you not to touch that thing," Angela said in between saying "Jesus Christ" repeatedly.

"You're washing me down the sink," I protested. My thumb felt almost numb except for the dull stinging.

"You are so stupid."

"I'm gonna all go down the drain," I repeated.

"You're not going to bleed to death, for Christ's sake," Angela said, gripping my wrist tighter as if she was trying to wring the blood out of my arm. She tucked her hair behind her ear impatiently and blew up into her bangs. "Someday you're going to bleed more than this. Every month. For years and years."

I started to cry. Angela was scaring me.

"No," I stuttered in denial.

Angela squeezed my thumb and a fresh gush of blood mixed with the water coming out of the tap. "This is what happens to stupid little girls who like fish. But I'm going to make it better. This isn't blood, it's all the bad poison in you. I'm cleaning it out for you."

I looked up into her face hopefully. "Really?"

I was saved by my mother's timely arrival home.

One stitch was all that was needed to close the wound. It looked like a black spider in the middle of my thumb. I picked at the black thread, hoping that Angela had got all the poison out before my skin started to heal over and sealed everything back inside. Eventually I forgot about the poison and started to cherish my scar, that pink worm bisecting my thumb as unique as the fingerprint it had altered, as if I needed extra proof that I wasn't like anyone else.

Washing my hands in the bathroom of my studio in Watson, I rub the scar on my thumb, caressing the familiar dent that has always symbolized a moment of rebellion that I've felt neither guilty nor proud of. Over the years the scar has become part of my identity, my thumb a one-of-a-kind.

I examine it under the light and wonder if it *is* the sealed exit point of some early poison. I shake my head and erase those thoughts. It's foolish to reopen old wounds.

To Angela, I add another "fuck off and die".

Later that evening, I go downstairs to Julie's studio and knock on the door. I'm sweating and my throat feels raw and fleshy from throwing up.

When Julie opens the door and sees me, her eyes widen for a moment then she breaks out into one of her big warm smiles.

"Hey, Anne. Come in, come in. I'm just making tea," she says, motioning me in ahead of her. The long kimono sleeves of her dress sweep the air in soft, graceful waves.

"One of your designs?" I say, pointing to her outfit.

"Uh-huh," she says, smoothing her hair down.

She has beautiful hair, shoulder length, honey colored with streaks of red. The dress is hand-painted silk, a subtle pattern of black and brown leaves on a background of dark mauve. She's wearing it like a tunic over copper colored shantung silk pants. She's tall, nearly as tall as Christian, and has a toned, yet voluptuous body, wide shoulders and a long elegant neck. She likes to wear flat slipper shoes, beautifully ornate with embroidery or beaded. Tonight she's wearing Aladdin slippers with turned up toes, woven with gold, copper and royal blue thread.

"It's gorgeous," I say. "And the shoes are very cool."

Julie smiles, looking me in the eye. "Sit," she says, pulling out a stool at her worktable. Pieces of silk are draped all over the top of the table, a colorful pile of art.

"What are you working on?" I say.

Julie turns from the sink where she's pouring hot water in a small Chinese teapot.

"I'm doing some costumes for the Kingston Theater Company. They're doing The King and I this season."

I finger a piece of silk by my elbow. My stomach muscles refuse to unclench.

"Must be nice to do such tactile work. Touching soft stuff all day."

"Ugh," Julie says, bringing the teapot and two cups over to the worktable. "There are days I'd kill for denim or canvas. Silk is so fussy and unforgiving. I once botched a jacket, using one of my fabrics and had to throw it out. Not like I could run down to FabricLand and buy some more."

"Guess you really have to plan out your moves ahead of time," I say.

Julie slides onto the stool across from me. "Yeah," she says, taking a sip of tea, her eyes watching me over the rim.

I look down in my cup, watching the brown tea leaves swimming in the bottom.

"I feel very awkward about the other night," I say.

"Awkward about what?" Julie says.

"Me, Christian. I'm sure it looked bad. I assure you nothing was going on. I was really drunk. He was just trying to get me home before I did anything embarrassing." My mouth goes into overdrive. "Well, I did do something embarrassing. You saw. I just... I wasn't... I wasn't trying to come on to him or anything. I know that's how it looked. Me throwing myself at Christian in the middle of Hunter Street."

Julie holds her hand up and I stop.

"Whoa," she says. "You don't owe me any explanations. I've been there. Gone out, let loose, then had to have someone carry me home. And from what I hear, you paid for it this morning. Wicked hangover. Been there." She shakes her head and picks up her teacup.

"You heard?"

She nods. "Christian was here for dinner. I promised him chicken satay a month ago. Had to pay up." She blushes and tucks her hair behind her ear.

"Oh," I say and feel the sweat on my neck dry.

"I don't think you're anything less than fabulous," Julie says, pouring more tea in my cup.

"Oh," I say again. "Phew." I pretend to wipe sweat off my forehead.

"So, Christian's been talking about doing a barbecue tomorrow night."

"On the beach?"

Julie nods. "Yup. Last one of the season. It's going to be a full moon."

Her eyes widen and she hugs her arms and pretends to shiver.

I smile and my stomach muscles finally relax.

I don't know what to think. I don't know what to do or what to feel. It's worse than I thought.

I had a portrait sitting this afternoon, a family wanting an official photograph with their new baby. But, this morning when I tested my light meter, it wasn't working. I figured I'd borrow August's.

I went to his door. It was open a few inches. I knocked once. There were no sounds from inside.

"August?" I said, sticking my head in the door.

There was movement in the bathroom, right behind the front door. I had a split-second glimpse of August quickly pulling a long sleeved t-shirt over his head, his back to me, then he turned around and walked out of the bathroom, raising his hand in a wave and moving past me into the kitchen.

"Hey, how's it going?" he said.

"Fine," I said. "I was wondering if I could—"

He turned around to open the fridge and when I saw his face, I forgot what I was going to say. He was wearing his hair loose instead of in a pony-tail, and it was hanging across his cheeks. It didn't quite hide the swelling at the corner of his mouth. There was a purple balloon on his bottom lip.

He grabbed a carton of milk out of the fridge and turned away from me, moving swiftly to the counter, pouring a cup of coffee from the percolator.

"I was wondering if I could borrow your light meter. What happened to your lip?"

He stood with his back to me, the milk carton clenched in his hand.

"Nothing," he said. "You want some coffee? I have to be at the reserve in an hour. New totem pole going up at the community center. They're doing a new brochure. Gotta have something for the printers by Tuesday. Then I have to do some shots of Lilly Crowfeather's shop for the insurance investigators. Roof got damaged in that windstorm last month. You want milk?"

He turned his head just enough to show his profile. I'd never seen him in such a hurry to do anything.

"I'm fine on the coffee. You okay?"

"I'm great," he said, keeping his back to me.

"Um, well... light meter?"

"On the table," he said, waving his arm.

I looked at the table. The only thing on it was a plate with half a piece of toast.

"This table?" I said.

Finally, he turned around. He looked at the table, his eyes darting back and forth. He ran his hand through his hair and I got a better look at his lip. There was a little bead of fresh blood on it.

"You're bleeding," I said, pointing to his mouth.

He licked his lip quickly, then hurried across the kitchen to his bedroom and knelt down by the bed, sticking his head under. "Ah, I have a spare meter here somewhere."

"August, if you can't find it, it's okay. I'll just wing it."

He stopped rummaging under his bed and went to shove himself back on his knees when the metal rail of the bed caught him on the back of his head, making a sickening sound.

"Ow," he yelled, holding the back of his head. He sat down heavily on the floor.

I ran over and dropped to my knees in front of him.

"Jesus, are you okay?"

"Ow," he said again.

"Let me see. You might have cut yourself."

I leaned over him and touched his hair, feeling a swelling lump on the curve of his skull.

"Man, you're having a rough day and it's only eleven o'clock."

August laughed, then stopped, his hand coming up to his mouth. "Shit," he said.

"Lemme see." I tilted his chin up. His lip was bleeding more. August's eyes flicked off of mine with embarrassment.

"You need some ice. You bite yourself?"

He jerked his head out of my hand, turning away. He stared at the night stand and the moment of silence grew until it was uncomfortable.

Then he moved suddenly, jumping to his feet. "I gotta go."

"August..." I said, getting up from the floor.

"Sorry about the light meter. I know it's here somewhere, but..."

"Were you in a fight or something?"

"I'm really late... I gotta..."

"Sorry. I'm not trying to be nosy."

He spun around and looked at me, his eyes dark. "She bit me, okay? It's stupid. It's embarrassing. It was an accident."

Maxine bit him? She was a hyper dog, liked to jump up on you.

"She's had all her shots, right?" I said.

August's face went slack for a second, then he flushed deep red. "Caroline," he said angrily. "Not Maxine."

I felt a hiccup in my throat and looked away, my face hot with embarrassment. "Oh," I said.

He heaved a quick sigh. "Sorry. Didn't mean to snap at you."

I couldn't look at him. I was trying not to picture under what circumstances Caroline might have bitten him. I was trying not to picture them together, tangled in passion.

"It's okay," I said, moving towards the door. "I gotta run too. Thanks anyway. Sorry about your head."

"Hey, Anne," August called when I was halfway out the door. "You coming to the barbecue tonight? Christian wanted to have the fire going by six."

"Yeah, sure," I said and ran down the hall to my studio.

I tried not to think about it all afternoon while I was doing the portrait of the young couple and their red-faced baby. August's embarrassment unsettled me. I'd stumbled over the ugly side of someone's privacy. I'd heard the cruelty and anger through the walls. I'd just never seen the evidence. I kept seeing the blood on August's lip. I felt the phantom pain on my mouth. It wasn't an accident. She had bitten him in anger. It made my heart sick.

The park is off Water Street and extends all the way from the street to the river. The grass just stops abruptly, the edge broken off at a little cliff. Below the cliff is a tiny band of sandy beach, then another band of rocks, then the river. The cliff has a small overhang that curves with the river to where the forest starts beside the park. That little curve of beach is the perfect place to have a barbecue. It's protected from the wind and it's private from the park and the street.

We have small parties here in the summer, usually just the four of us from The Factory, sometimes Mia and her sometimes boyfriend, Raymond. Caroline has never come.

Christian, as usual is acting host, building the fire, bringing blankets to sit on, planning the menu (burgers and potatoes). It's kind of cold for a barbecue, but it will be the last one before winter. We build a bigger fire to stay warm.

I part enjoy and part fear these outdoor adventures. I'm a city girl. It gets really dark in a rural town at night. I'm convinced the people who grew up here have better night vision. I'm just overwhelmed by the blackness, and at the same time I'm awed by the power of nature. It's humbling not to be able to turn on a light switch.

The forest beside the park is particularly sinister. The leaf trees are almost stripped bare like skeletons, yet the pines and cedars are still dense enough that the forest is thick and shadowy, able to hide large creatures.

It's an excited fear I have, tempted by the brutality of being out in the open. I know I'm safe with my friends, and yet there's always a potential danger lurking. I want to feel stronger outside near the forest. I may have to rely on my instincts, like a pioneer, fight off a bear or survive on roots and berries.

I would never admit these things out loud. To Christian, Julie and August, this is just an activity, a break from work.

We're all standing around the fire, too cold to sit down.

"Should we have the marshmallows first?" Julie says, fishing the bag out of Christian's cooler.

"It's not even dark yet," Christian says, waving smoke out of his face.

The sky is hedging against twilight, a sea of navy above the black water of the river. Christian keeps throwing more kindling on the fire, concerned that we're all cold.

August is scouring the shoreline for bricks. I watch his dark figure, bent over, his hair falling over his face. In the fading light his green corduroy coat looks like velvet.

"But you're supposed to have dessert first when you have a barbecue," Julie says, squishing the marshmallows through the package with her thumb.

Christian straightens up from fanning the fire, puts his hands on his hips and gives her an impatient look, then grins. "Knock yourself out, but you'd better eat your burger later or I'm feeding it to the beavers."

Julie is wearing a bulky blue turtleneck under her beige canvas barn jacket. She looks outdoorsy and fashionable.

When August wanders back over to the fire, Julie smiles at him and offers him a marshmallow.

"Find any bricks?" she says.

August shakes his head. Julie watches him put a marshmallow in his mouth. Then she turns to me. She gives me a questioning look. She's noticed August's fat lip.

I lick my lips and look away.

We eat and drink beer, sitting on blankets close to the fire. The sky has transformed into a planetarium, a blue ceiling dotted with lights. August's arm shoots out, pointing to a falling star we all look too late to see.

Christian is entertaining us with stories about the construction project he's working on, a new subdivision of twenty houses in Lakefield. The contractor is addicted to Nintendo.

"He carries that fucking Gameboy all over the site," Christian says. "Playing incessantly, like he can't stop. And of course he's not watching where he's going so he's always stepping in dog shit, tripping over wheel barrels, doing the Wile E. Coyote with two by fours, whacking himself in the head."

August loves that one, falling over on his side laughing.

"So Thursday...." Christian says, warming up to the story. "He walks right into a bucket of wet cement and drops his Gameboy, plop, right in the bucket. Man you should have heard him. 'My game! My game!' Offered one guy twenty bucks to stick his hand in and fish it out. We were all killing ourselves laughing, watching the cement dry, entombing his precious Nintendo. The rest of the day he's walking around just lost, going crazy without it."

We're all laughing now. Julie is giggling and grabbing Christian's arm.

Christian suddenly looks serious. "By five o'clock, he was so pathetic we all started feeling sorry for him. We took up a collection and went and bought him a new one. One of the guys poured the old one in with the cement into the foundation. That house is going to be special. I wouldn't be surprised if Mario buys the place himself so he can be close to his Gameboy."

"Wile E. Coyote!" August says, still laughing about the two by four in the head.

Christian gets up to throw another log on the fire. "Hey, August. Tell us one of your Indian ghost stories."

August pokes a stick in the fire and pulls it out, then blows on the glowing ember at the tip. "Have I told you guys the one about my Uncle Leonard?"

Julie looks at Christian. They both shrug. Christian looks at me. I shake my head.

August is still blowing on the end of his stick. He starts to smile slowly. "Good. You're going to like this one."

I've never actually heard the story, though August never fails to mention that his Uncle Leonard is the one "who had his finger bitten off by a bear."

August tells good stories. His voice gets low, kind of sexy, and his face stays expressionless, forcing you to focus on his words.

I get scared and feel silly. The story ends with someone seeing a bear with a human finger growing out of its paw.

I drink too much beer and have to pee. I hold off as long as I can, dreading the thought of having to go in the forest behind some black bony tree.

When I can't hold it any longer I get up.

"Okay, nature is calling in a big way."

Julie discreetly hands me a few serviettes.

"Me too," August says, getting up.

"An escort, Anne. You should be honored," Christian says.

"Watch out for coyotes," Julie says. Christian throws a marshmallow at her and she gives a throaty giggle.

"It's the beavers you have to watch for," Christian says, his face serious. "They'll eat your underwear."

He and Julie start laughing and throwing marshmallows at each other. As August and I walk towards the trees, their laughter carries over the water echoing off the opposite bank.

We walk into the forest quite far. Once the trees envelop us it's pitch black and suffocating. The darkness becomes a soft wall touching me all over. I keep my eyes on August, walking ahead of me, sure-footed, graceful. I keep stumbling over rocks and roots.

"Now why didn't anybody think to bring a flashlight?" I say.

August turns around, but I can't make out his face. Then he smiles and a thin beam of light illuminates his face. He's holding a penlight under his chin.

"You couldn't have turned that on a few minutes ago?" I say.

August flicks the light on and off, his face disappearing and reappearing. My breath catches every time he turns the light off.

"Here," August says, handing me the flashlight. "That tree has your name on it."

He points out a tree for me and disappears into the forest to my right.

It's quiet, except for the crickets. The wind ripples through the pines like a giant sighing. I put the penlight down on the ground and immediately the light starts to fade. It grows fainter and fainter, then dies completely.

"Damn," I whisper.

"I can hear you peeing," August calls out.

I'm glad to hear his voice even if I can't see him. We're still connected in the dark.

"If I get poison ivy, I'll make you pay," I yell.

"You'll be too busying scratching," he yells back.

I laugh. A wave of wind roars through the trees and when it's gone there are no sounds. I finish peeing and stand up, looking around me blindly. I don't hear anything. No twigs snapping. No sound of August moving through the trees.

I walk back to where we parted. It's so black everything is flat, dense, and cold. I'm getting scared. Another wave of wind is coming. I can hear it building in the trees further back in the forest, a whispering roar growing louder, drowning out all the little sounds I'm straining to hear. The wave reaches me, blowing my hair forward into my face, parting it in the back of my head like an invisible comb.

I'm turning around in circles, looking left, right, forward, behind. The trees are so tall I can't see the sky. I take a few steps, stop, take a few more and stop. I can't see August anywhere. I stop and listen. Nothing.

"August?" I'm starting to freak out. I can feel the forest behind me, breathing down my neck. "Where are you? I can't see anything."

Silence. I can't hear him anywhere.

I start walking faster. Dead ferns wrap around my ankles, trying to trip me. Low branches hit me in the chest.

I feel really claustrophobic. I don't want to yell or scream. I feel stupid, but I'm genuinely afraid.

I run a few steps and see an opening, some sort of path that's clear of trees. It's not so dark on the path, so I break into a jog. Then suddenly there's a dark shape in the middle of the path ahead of me, low to the ground. Before I can stop, it moves.

I gasp and exhale an embarrassing little squeak.

It's August. He stands up and turns around just as I'm clutching my hands to my chest.

"Look what I found," he says, excited, holding out his hand. "Wintergreen. For dessert."

"You scared the shit out of me," I say, ignoring the leaves in his hand.

"You're scared?"

"It's really spooky in here. And your stupid flashlight ran out of batteries," I say, trying to sound angry and brave.

August smiles. I just see his white teeth.

I walk past him. I want to be in front on the way out. He can let the forest breathe down his neck.

He's close behind me as I wade through some pine trees. The needles feel like silk on my hand.

"Wait," August says.

I stop and he stops right behind me.

"Listen," he whispers, holding me still by the shoulders. "Close your eyes and listen."

I close my eyes and tilt my head back. I can hear him breathing, feel his fingers pressing into my arms. I lean back a bit into his chest. His jacket is soft. I can smell him, earthy and warm. The air is heavy with the smell of leaves and pine needles. His chest is solid against my back. My body relaxes against him, and he puts his arms loosely around me, pulling me closer. He turns his head and his cheek touches my ear, his skin cool and soft.

"You see. There's nothing to be scared of," he says. "Keep your eyes closed."

Then he lets go of my arms and I feel like a disciple, surrendering their fear before baptism. I stand alone, eyes closed, listening to the wind in the trees, dry trunks creaking and groaning, soft whispers, gentle, peaceful. I'm getting into it, my face up to the stars, standing still like a tree, pretending I'm part of the forest. I smile.

When I open my eyes and look around, he's gone. I can't believe he moved that quietly. It's really dark and I become aware of being alone, frighteningly so.

I start to run. I know I'm not far from the beach. I can see the sky opening up ahead over the park.

I stumble and flail through the trees. And then I hear August laughing. He's up ahead, right at the edge of the forest, leaning against a tree waiting for me.

"You asshole," I yell, but I'm laughing now.

I grab him as I run past and we fall out of the forest into the open air of the park.

We run right across to the other side, laughing, weaving around trees and picnic tables, me chasing August, him chasing me.

When we're winded we stop, face to face, bent over, hands on our knees trying to catch our breath.

August straightens up. His face has gone serious, watching me as if he's preparing to say something.

I look at his mouth, the red lump on his lip.

He sees me looking and licks his lips, turning his head away.

I open my mouth to speak.

"Don't," he says, shaking his head.

"Okay," I say.

We stand still for a moment listening to the wind, the rush of the river, Christian and Julie's voices drifting up from the beach.

August knows that I know. It wasn't an accident. I've wandered into his forest, into the scary pines, and learned this secret.

I feel the heat. I'm walking deeper into the fire.

CHAPTER FIVE

Photographic Memory

I keep a mental image of the photographs I've taken. With my old work locked away in my mother's attic, the photos in my head are all I have. The work I've done in the last year has no history. It was shot by someone else. Not the Albertine Hannah who spent years in Toronto building a portfolio that chronicled an artist's life.

Lately, before I fall asleep, I've been doing this recall thing. Not all the pictures I've taken, just the ones that were in my last show. I mentally walk through the gallery, stand before one photo at a time.

I get stuck every time I get to the one... the *offensive* one. I skip over it. I know it better than the rest, don't I? I had to look at it everyday in court, hear it described in the newspaper, on television. I feel like a coward for stemming my affection for that photo. I thought it was so beautiful when I took it. Then I lost my objectivity.

The photograph was titled In *The Arms Of Daniel*.

I say 'was' because it does not exist anymore, print, negative or otherwise.

Daniel was one of the models, a dancer. I got the idea while shooting him and Eric, who was also a dancer, and Daniel's lover.

Daniel and Eric were horsing around in my studio while I was changing the film in my camera. I was taking shots of them for a poster advertising their dance company's upcoming production. I had them leaping around, twirling and bending, contrasting their choreography, one in motion, the other still, one high, the other low. I got some great shots that captured the action and drama of modern dance. I thought I might get a few more in black and white. It was getting late. I was tired, they were tired. Not too tired to play, though.

They were like two lion cubs, teasing, laughing, poking, chasing each other around. Then suddenly I heard them stop, their feet still, the sound of their breathing and sighing filling the studio. I looked up from my camera and caught a pure spontaneous moment between them.

Daniel was hugging Eric from behind. It was the first time all day I'd seen them touch not as dancers, but as people. As I watched, Daniel laid his cheek in the curve of Eric's shoulder, pulling him into a closer embrace. They both closed their eyes. The moment their bodies found the right grooves in each other was like a puzzle that had been put back together.

I'd caught them perfectly out of pose.

Daniel opened his eyes and saw me looking. He didn't move. He just smiled, a lazy, self-satisfied smile.

"Are you tired?" I asked.

Eric nodded without opening his eyes. They looked like a split-time version of Gemini, Daniel the mature full grown twin, Eric the one caught in an adolescent transition.

There was an interesting contrast in their style of dancing. Eric had a lithe grace, while Daniel was the strong man, the Atlas to Eric's world. Daniel was tall, his physique, hard and muscular, a rippling chest and bronze-skinned perfection. His face was beautiful, a square chin, light blue eyes and a full head of black curly hair. He was almost too perfect, a modern day Greek god, his expression charming, confident, yet sensitive.

I admit, as a photographer, I love the human body. I love perfect proportion, flawless skin, graceful movement, the power that emanates from an inner knowledge of physical beauty. And yet I love equally the unique physique that has some oddity or flaw.

Eric standing next to Daniel looked like his protégé, a few steps behind, shorter by a head, his chest small, no waist or hips, all lean and raw, only hints of his dancer's muscle in his thighs. His hands and feet were over sized, incongruous lumps of knuckles and toes attached to delicate wrists and ankles. He had a waif-like face, the mink gray color and texture of his brush cut showing an aching innocence at the nape of his neck. And yet, despite what their physiques might have conveyed about their personalities – Eric's innocence to Daniel's worldliness – if you looked closer, you noticed the street tough in Eric; his steely eyes, clenched jaw, skinned knuckles, and nicotine-stained fingers. Daniel gave away his tenderness when he spoke, his voice high-pitched and soft, as if he were afraid to offend. Eric's voice was low and gravely, and he liked to use the word "fuck" as a noun, adjective and verb.

Daniel's love softened Eric's wildness. Beauty taming the beast. That's what I found so interesting about photographing them. I wanted to capture that rare kind of affection, the loving hand of Daniel reaching out to tame Eric.

And so I said, in that stilled moment of witnessing them perfectly out of pose, "If you're tired, you can lay down on the bed over there." I had a bed behind a screen. I sometimes slept at my studio.

I think Daniel knew what I was after. He moved Eric over to the bed, like a sleep walker, guiding him by his arms. Eric kept his eyes closed, laughing like it was a game.

I got my camera off the tripod. They'd used a ladder as a prop for the shoot and I moved it quickly and quietly up to the screen. I didn't want to stir them out of the mood.

Just when I was worrying about the light, one of them turned on the floor lamp beside the bed. It was so quiet in there. I grabbed my camera and climbed the ladder.

I was surprised by what I saw when I looked over the top of the screen. Daniel had removed Eric's clothes and was in the process of taking off his own leotard. He was moving slowly, like he was slipping into bed and didn't want to wake Eric. I was about to protest that I hadn't wanted them naked, just resting. But then Daniel rolled over on his side, molding himself up against Eric's back. He slipped his arms around him and settled in. Eric laughed again. He had his eyes closed, like it was still a game.

They both sighed, relaxing, thigh to buttock, chest to back, chin to neck. God, it was an unbelievable picture. I snapped it before I could think too much.

I took four shots, one after the other, praying there was enough light. I was sweating, my hands twitching with excitement. How often does a photographer get their models to do something so natural? It was like suddenly they were unaware I was there, had lapsed so easily into their own private world and there I was on top of a ladder looking down at this beautiful scene through the lens of my camera.

When I finished shooting Daniel and Eric, I climbed off the ladder, tiptoed around the screen and pulled the blanket over them. Then I switched off the lamp by the bed.

"Good night," Daniel whispered.

I left them a key to lock up, crept out of the studio and drove home, my hands on the steering wheel beating with adrenaline.

I didn't have a chance to develop the shots for a week. Another assignment came up and kept me away from the darkroom.

As soon as I was free, I got busy printing. I pulled the shots of Eric and Daniel out of the final bath and felt a buzz of excitement. When they were dry, I took them into the light. I knew right away they were better than good.

The square of the bed framed the picture, the white sheets all dunes and valleys where they were rumpled.

The light and shadow was incredible. Since I'd shot them in black and white, their bodies seemed composed not of arms and legs, but of circles and oblongs, all grainy and soft like ripples of sand in a desert landscape.

Daniel's thigh and shoulder had ovals of white on the surface, the bottom edge of his jaw tilting up in a line of gray, paralleled by the darker ridge of his right eyebrow. Below that black line, the light hit Daniel's eye, which was open and staring at the back of Eric's neck. His right arm and hand disappeared over Eric's body, then the tops of his knuckles reappeared next to Eric's stomach. The tip of Eric's penis was visible, a small pale dome and though Daniel's hand was resting beside it, a blur of gray connected them in the dark.

The fuzzy shadows flowed in variations of light gray, soft black and hard black, forming soft crevices between their bodies where they dipped together.

Eric looked wrapped in cloth by the shadow of Daniel's body. But his face was tilted up and the light hit his nose, his chin, and the curve of his mouth, while the thin black line of his eye, made him look like he had it squeezed shut or he was squinting. His legs and feet mingled with Daniel's in extreme shadow, the top of his hip a darker reflection of Daniel's. In between the two curving lines where the edges of their bodies met, there was a series of shadow shapes, a pale circle, a gray oval, floating in soft black.

The oddest thing was, that in all the lack of definition, the fuzzy shapes of their limbs and torsos, Eric's arm was curled over Daniel's, and the angle of light thrown from the lamp beside the bed fell right on his hand. I hadn't noticed it when I snapped the picture, but Eric had his hand up to his mouth and was sucking his thumb.

There is always a point of focus in a photograph. It's not necessarily the object in the center or even the largest thing. In my photograph, Eric's hand was the focal point, the one detailed thing rising up out of a pool of milky water. Something about the innocence of his pose, sucking his thumb like a contented child both thrilled and unnerved me. I loved the incongruity, the thumb sucking with the naked male bodies, and I felt daring holding the picture.

No one could have posed that naturally. I thought about how much of it was just pure luck on my part – right place, right time. I'd worn them out dancing and then been around to catch that moment when their bodies quit acting. And there they lay in that stilled moment, spooning as only willing lovers do.

I called both of them and asked if I could use the shots of them sleeping.

"Do we look pretty?" Daniel asked.

"You're gorgeous," I assured him.

"Then by all means," he said.

Daniel actually did see the photograph right before it went on display. He was over at my studio and asked about it. When he saw it, he jokingly said, "God, it looks like we're fucking."

I had an upcoming show. I'd already picked all the photos I wanted in it, but at the last minute I framed the best one of my sleeping lovers. In retrospect, I shouldn't have altered my plans.

My gallery show consisted of a series of photos I'd taken the year before at The Maple Leaf Steam Baths on Bathurst Street. The subjects were old men, some sitting in groups in the lounge, towels around their sagging waists, exposing soft, caved-in chests, graying hair, gnarled hands and feet. Some of the photos were group shots in the baths themselves, steam clouding the air, old men smiling in the pool, some sitting on the side, an unselfconscious kinship in displaying their aged bodies amongst old friends who they'd probably known when their bodies were young and hard.

So what was I thinking putting the photo of Daniel and Eric in with the old men from the steam bath? I honestly don't know. I remember thinking that I was a little tired of the Maple Leaf Steam Bath photos because they were a year old and I had this urge to include something recent. I thought Daniel and Eric fit in with the general theme of male nudes. I didn't think for one minute that a perceived age difference would be the crowbar the law used to widen the gap between consenting adult and innocent child.

See, here's what I *should* have done. I should have had an entire exhibit of just Daniel and Eric. Not just them sleeping, but dancing, leaping around, in the light, where there could be no mistake as to who they were.

I drifted up from a deep pool of sleep the morning after the barbecue, aware that I'd heard a sound, but not sure if it was in my dreams. Far off, I thought I heard someone calling my name. In my dreams I heard "Albertine". As I surfaced, the voice changed and I sat up with a start, realizing it was saying "Anne".

I looked across the room, blinking. August had his head in the door and I could see his mouth moving. "Anne," he said.

I jumped out of bed, my heart pounding. "What's wrong?" I said.

August opened the door and walked in, his hands up. "Nothing. Everything's okay. I thought I heard something fall."

I took a step and stubbed my toe on something sharp. I looked down and saw my alarm clock lying on the floor, one corner chipped off.

"Guess you really didn't want to get up this morning," August said.

I plopped down on the edge of the bed, my toe throbbing. "What time is it?"

August looked at his watch. "Ten sixteen."

"Oh, shit," I said, jumping up again. "I was supposed to help Julie deliver some bolts of fabric this morning." I grabbed the phone beside the bed and began punching in numbers.

"You want some coffee?" August said.

"Sure."

"Toast?" he said, moving around the kitchen.

"Sure," I said, listening to Julie's phone ring.

I watched August, wondering what was going on. It was there, some kind of subtle shift in the tenor of our friendship.

I was off the hook with Julie. The store she was supposed to deliver material to was closed today because the manager was sick. She asked me if I could help her at the end of the week.

While August hummed and got intimate with my kitchen, I closed the bathroom door behind me and turned to face the mirror over the sink.

The edges of my dreams were still clinging, dividing me between asleep and awake, reality and fiction, lies and truth.

I gripped the edges of the sink with both hands and looked at my face in the mirror. I had a sudden impulse to run into the other room and tell August my real name. I saw myself saying it. "I'm Albertine Hannah." I pinched the inside of my arm to wake myself up. What if I couldn't control myself? What if I just blurted it out sometime? Jesus, I was leaking around the edges.

"Anne Hanes," I said to my reflection. My face was fierce.

And then I scrubbed my face until my skin burned. I brushed my teeth until my gums bled. After, I felt raw and tough. I spat blood in the sink, turned on the tap and washed it clean away.

"Butter?" August said, taking the toast out of the toaster oven.

My toaster oven is broken, the swinging door held down with a heavy metal name plate that says "Acme" on it. Christian found it for me at a junk store. He found the toaster oven, too.

"Yeah," I said, standing beside August at the counter.

He buttered the toast with great precision, scraping the knife into each corner. I got mesmerized watching him.

He put the toast on a plate and slid it over to me, leaning closer at the same time. I looked at the toast. August's head was close to mine.

"Your hair still smells like smoke," he said.

"So does yours," I said, turning my face towards him. Only he hadn't turned away yet, and we bumped noses.

"Sorry," I said, laughing. His face was blurry up close, a soft plane of skin marked by the red blur of his mouth.

Something else, August's hand was resting on top of mine on the counter.

He moved his head up, his chin moving past my eye. Then I felt his lips on my forehead, not a kiss, just his lips resting there, like his hand on top of mine.

It seemed like we stood there for a long time, his mouth resting on my forehead, his hand on top of mine, the smell of smoke coming off of us. The cuckoo clock in August's studio suddenly bonged and broke the moment. We moved apart.

August walked over to the table and stood looking at my bedroom.

"You finally unpacked," he said.

"Yeah."

"You've decided to stay?" He said it with a smile, but his eyes looked at me steadily.

I looked away. The imprint of his lips was still warm on my forehead. "Um... I don't know. Maybe. I figured at the very least I should be a *neat* visitor."

August nodded slowly. "Right," he said. "So, there's something I wanted your advice on."

I picked up the toast and took a bite. "Was' that?" I said, with my mouth full.

"I've been thinking of putting some of my photographs in a gallery."

I swallowed quickly. "Where?"

"In Ottawa," he said. "They want me to have a show next month."

My skin got electric. I remembered my shows in Toronto, friends' shows, the glitter and drama, the music and black leather jackets, the smoky air and bad wine, bodies crammed together, too loud to talk, the excitement like a drug, the atmosphere urban thin, so hip it hurt, painfully cool and detached, the glory, God, the glory of being at the center of it all.

"When did you —" I started to say. "How did all this come about?"

"I sent them some pictures a few months ago. Remember the

ones I did of the fire? They sent me a letter and asked for more, then they called last week and I said I'd do it."

August walked over to the counter and poured himself some coffee. I handed him the carton of milk.

"Wow..." I said. "That's great. So what do you need advice on?"

August looked in his coffee cup. "I wanted to know if you think I should do it."

"Sure. Yeah. Why not?"

August tilted his head and squinted. "Caroline's not that keen on the idea. She thinks I'm not ready. That I'm just setting myself up for disappointment."

"August, if you weren't ready, the gallery wouldn't want you."

"I don't know," he said. "I've never had a gallery show other than Curve Lake."

"What's the name of the gallery in Ottawa?"

August raised his eyebrows. "Kronos. Ever heard of it?"

Yeah, I'd heard of it. It was one of the hippest galleries in the capital city. They had a reputation for breaking hot new artists.

I nodded. "It's pretty well known."

A nervous look crossed August's face. "Oh boy," he said. "Why do they want me?"

"Because you're good, that's why."

He lowered his head and I could see him choosing his words carefully. "You think I'm ready?"

I looked at the mark on his lip. The swelling had gone down and left a smooth red bump.

"Yes. I do," I said.

While I title my pictures, August dates his. I don't mean just the day, month, year. He also records the exact time he took the picture, right down to the seconds. He has one of those digital watches specifically for that purpose.

Later that night, while sorting through photographs on August's kitchen table, I felt humbled. You didn't learn to be that good through schooling. August was born a great photographer. In his pictures, I saw the confidence that allows risk. His photographs of the Dominion Foods fire were breathtaking. The drama in his pictures threw heat off the paper and the smell of smoke. His use of light and his sense of composition were so artistic. I kept looking at him as we sat at the table silently putting 'possibles' in a pile, wondering how many more unexpected layers existed under the surface.

I pictured each photograph framed, hanging on a white wall, a little white card underneath that would read something like, "November 6th–Wednesday–5:42:16 a.m.". And I was picturing August milling around a crowded gallery, a glass of wine in his hand, wearing his blue Muskoka dinner jacket with his black Underdog t-shirt underneath, his jeans and muddy sneakers, his face flushed with cold as if he'd just wandered into the gallery from a long walk in the woods. How would they see him? An eccentric artist? An eccentric *Aboriginal* artist. His exotic features would add to his mystery. Yes, I could see it. Women would think he was beautiful. Men would envy his sensitivity.

He would knock their socks off.

The next morning I woke up with the sunrise coming in my window, my dreams still buzzing in my arms and legs. I ate break-fast standing at the counter, too antsy to sit down. My dreams were full of people and places. There were parties, dark rooms filled with noise, music and laughter, and I was excited to be there, like I'd just woken from a coma and wanted to catch up on everything I'd missed.

I looked at the four walls of my studio and felt an urge to escape. Out the window, wind was blowing the trees back and forth, scattering leaves. A cloud sped across the sun, and then a quilted carpet rolled across the ceiling of the sky.

Next door, August's stereo came on. Billie Holiday's little girl alto, melancholy and slow. I heard Maxine bark, then the skitter of her nails across the floor.

I had to get out of there.

As soon as I opened the closet to get my coat, someone knocked on the door, rapping sharply on the glass. It startled me.

I recognized her shape behind the bubbled glass. Something about the way she moved her head, an impatience to get where she was going.

I opened the door. "Hey," I said.

"Hi, Anne," Caroline said, and without stopping, walked in the door.

I backed up and smiled at her. Caroline had been different since her photo shoot. Friendlier, as if we'd shared a confidence.

"I see you're an early riser like me. Heard you get up and then I smelled coffee." Her eyes widened on the word 'coffee'.

"You want some?" I said. "It's coffeemaker."

"Love some," she said, and then I noticed the coffee cup in her hand. "August forgot to buy beans. Again." She rolled her eyes at me.

I took the cup from her and went into the kitchen.

Caroline raised her shoulders, lacing her fingers together in front. "So what are you up to on this gorgeous fall day?"

"Not sure," I said. "How 'bout you?"

"Oh, just a few errands." Her voice came from my bedroom and I turned around and saw her tilt her head to read the book titles on my night stand.

I walked over and handed her the coffee cup, then went back to the kitchen. I couldn't figure out why she was here. Was it just to borrow a cup of coffee or were we going to sit at the table, tell secrets and engage in some female bonding?

I stood at the counter and waited.

Caroline continued to browse my book selection, sipping her coffee, picking up items on the night stand, checking out the poster on the wall over the bed, seeming unaware that a profoundly awkward silence had existed for several minutes.

I got desperate and spoke. "So how's Maxine?"

Caroline smiled slowly. "She's great."

I nodded. A half minute passed. "And how's business?"

Caroline was checking out the pile of camera equipment in the corner. Her expression was more like she was looking at a pile of greasy car parts. "Fa-bu-lous," she said. "I just wish I could get August as fired up about something. He's still in bed."

"I guess he's been busy thinking about going to Ottawa," I said.

Caroline's head swung around to look at me. "Yeah, I wanted to talk to you about that."

"Oh?"

"Yeah." She walked over to me and when she spoke again, her voice was low and urgent. "I'd appreciate it if you didn't encourage this crazy idea about the art gallery."

I shrugged. "I guess I don't think it's such a crazy idea."

She tilted her head and studied me for a moment. "You don't know him like I do, Anne. How fragile he is. I think it's sweet you share this interest in cameras, but..." She lifted her shoulder and held it there. "Don't get him believing he's something he's not. He's not equipped to handle that kind of scrutiny. If it doesn't go well, he'll be crushed."

I struggled for a response.

Caroline was looking at me pleadingly. "I don't want to see him get hurt."

The irony was too much. I closed my eyes and shook my head.

"Good," Caroline said. "We agree. Thanks for the coffee." She looked at her watch. "I've really got to run."

I leaned against the counter and watched her walk out the door, her stride confident. Business settled. Mission accomplished.

I really had to get out of there.

I walked down to The Terminal Diner, hoping Mia was working today. I needed some normal conversation to wash the recent one out of my ears.

All the way down George Street, a jumble of words bounced around in my head. I couldn't complete a thought. One started, then jumped tracks and I wanted to break into a run just to escape them.

By the time I turned the corner onto King Street, I was walking so fast, my shins were cramping up. I looked at the metal facade of the diner, then across the street to the bus terminal. Without stopping, I crossed the street and walked into the lobby of the bus terminal.

Twenty minutes later I was sitting on a bus bound for Toronto.

CHAPTER SIX

The Missing Photograph

I watched as farmland gave way to strip malls on the outskirts of Oshawa, the evolution of my rural life back into the urban landscape I had grown up with taking place with each revolution of the bus wheels. I wondered what the hell I was doing.

I pulled my wallet out of my knapsack and took out my driver's license. I looked at my name underneath my picture. *Albertine Hannah*, and underneath was my tiny signature. I hadn't signed that name in nearly a year. I wondered if I still knew how.

A half hour later, I was standing outside the Toronto Bus Depot at the corner of Dundas and Bay, deep in the heart of downtown. I'd forgotten how big everything was. The buildings towered over the street, cars rushed past, sirens wailed, horns honked, and the sheer volume of people hurrying along the sidewalks was like a film in fast motion. A young couple with backpacks bumped into me, rushing out the door of the terminal to catch a taxi. If I didn't keep moving, I was going to be knocked over.

I walked along Dundas to Yonge Street, the center of the universe, and stood on the southwest corner in front of the Eaton Centre, the mall that was an entire city block long. I looked up and down Yonge, at the new mega Gap store on the opposite corner, further up the giant swirling wheel of neon in front of Sam The Record Man. Behind me a bag lady was yelling at a businessman in a five hundred dollar Hugo Boss suit. In front of the revolving doors to the mall, an old man sat on a milk crate, playing a harmonica, tossing his head back and forth. Across the street, a midget in an ink-stained apron stood in front of his newspaper stand, watching people walk by. He caught me staring and saluted. I saluted back.

Then someone knocked me in the shoulder. I looked around and saw a skinny boy in jeans and a Maple Leafs jacket standing at my elbow.

"You need anything?" he mumbled, his eyes darting around.

I kept looking at him.

"Angel dust? Acid? Pot?"

I shook my head and headed towards the entrance to the subway.

I took the Yonge subway line up to Bloor Street, transferred trains and went along Bloor till it turned into Danforth Avenue. I got off at the Chester Station and walked up Jackman to Browning. Then I was turning onto my mother's street.

I stood in front of the weathered oak door, still bearing the patch of dents at the bottom where Arvo had kicked it with his ice skates.

"Com-ing, com-ing," I heard my mother calling in a high voice from inside.

The door swung open, her face froze for a second, then her mouth opened in surprise.

"Oh my goodness where did you come from?" she said, grinning. Before I could answer, she pulled me in the door and stood me in front of her. "Yes, I think you're my daughter. It's been awhile, but..." She pursed her lips and tapped her finger on them. "Hmm... Yes, you're her." She took my hands and squeezed them.

"Hi, Mum," I said.

"You just got on a bus?" my mother said, coming to sit at the table across from me.

Her kitchen had been repainted, a modern hue of light green I assumed was Angela's doing. She'd gotten a new fridge with an ice-maker in the door.

"Yeah," I said, tearing my eyes away from the burn mark on the floor by the stove. I'd dropped a cake pan when I was ten and it melted the vinyl tile before I could find the potholder. "Just felt like a visit, so I hopped on a Greyhound this morning."

"What would you like for lunch?" my mother said, jumping up from the table. "Cheese melts with bacon?"

"Oh, boy," I said.

"You can stay in your old room tonight," she said, watching me eat. "Your bed's all made up."

"Sure. That would be great."

"So tell me what you've been doing," she said, resting her elbows on the table.

The weirdness of being back in Toronto was just starting to lift when I heard the front door open and a second later, "Hell-oo-oo. I'm here."

My mother touched my hand and smiled. "We're in here," she called.

Angela walked into the kitchen carrying a large shopping bag. "We who?" She saw me and stopped, the bag crinkling loudly as she put it down on the floor. "Well, this is a big surprise," she said.

"She just hopped on a Greyhound this morning," my mother said in a cheery voice.

"Is she back for good?" Angela said, staring as if she was afraid to take her eyes off me.

"She has to be back tomorrow," I said. "How you been, Ange?"

"Super," she said. "And you?"

"Oh, same old. Been working on my Ph.D. and trying solve the problem of global warming."

She tried to stop it, but I made her laugh.

"Is there enough tea left for me?" she said, moving over to a chair.

"I'll get you a cup, dear," my mother said, getting up and going into the dining room.

Angela and I sat listening to the sound of the china cabinet door opening, then the delicate rattle of teacups. My mother always used the good china when we had tea.

"You want the red one with flowers or the green and gold one?" my mother called from the dining room.

Angela looked at me, and our eyes connected. "Green," she said without looking away.

Long past midnight, I lay on top of the comforter on my old bed, staring at the ceiling. Headlights moved across the wall every once in a while, and in the distance was the screech and groan of a streetcar rounding the corner at Broadview and Danforth.

It was like waking from a coma. The past year was a blur, a loop of events someone had tied together, the loop disappearing, the ends reconnecting, creating a seamless bridge across a gap where I had pretended to be someone else.

My mother sent me out for bread the next morning. While I was waiting my turn at the bakery, I saw a familiar pile of newspapers by the door and went to get one.

Exit was the magazine I freelanced for when I lived in Toronto. Every city has one, a hip weekly paper that features young writers, a guide to what music is playing, and reviews of books, dance and art. I'd supplied Exit with photos for three years and they'd covered my trial. I missed the place. I'd done some of my best work for them.

Their offices were just a few blocks from my mother's, down on Danforth Avenue.

When I got back to my mother's, I called my old friend, Irene, who was the photo editor at Exit, just a social call to see how she'd been.

She was really surprised to hear from me. Okay, I glossed over some things. Said I'd been working up north for a while, that I was really busy, happy, and that I didn't miss Toronto. She asked me to drop by for a visit. I almost said no, but my mother, who was standing there, eavesdropping, started nodding her head and poking me in the back, so I said yes.

I went by at 6:30, after most of the staff had gone for the day. Irene and I talked for a long time. The energy of deadlines still hung in the air and the smell of newsprint made me nostalgic for a simpler time in my life. We talked about people we knew, crazy assignments we'd done. We didn't talk about the trial or my disappearance from Toronto.

After I left, I realized how little validation I'd had in the past year. Spending two and a half hours with someone calling me Albertine had a strange effect on me. I'd focused on one short segment of my history for so long, I'd neglected all the great stuff that happened before. Irene knew me, knew my successes, and the breadth and depth of my career.

She asked me to send some of my recent work, anything I thought the magazine might be interested in using. She even asked if I wanted to go out on assignments. I told her I wasn't moving back to Toronto, but I gave her my phone number in Watson and in doing so, I made my first link with the outside world in nearly a year.

The buzz of the city energized me in a way I missed. A lot was the same, the rudeness and impatience of people in stores, insane traffic and psychotic drivers, and the landmarks, the CN Tower, the SkyDome, the elegance of the old City Hall were unchanged, but everything held a freshness for me after being away so long. I had changed. The Toronto that had existed in my mind for the past year was a stagnant pool of bad memories. Seeing it in person, I realized the city had swallowed the past and moved on.

That afternoon, I took the streetcar along Queen to Spadina, the heart of the garment district, and the funky bohemian neighborhood where I'd lived and had my studio. It hadn't changed much, still lots of cool cafes and clothing boutiques mixed in with original greasy spoons and fabric stores. The Horseshoe Tavern, once an honest-to-God country bar, then a punk bar, and now the premier host of alt-rock music, sat as unassuming as ever on the north side of the street. On the south side was the tall stately building with a glassed roundhouse on the third floor. It took me back a few years, to the height of the artists' invasion along Queen Street West. A painter named Dallas Bennett had lived in that building with his mother and his sister, Rory. Rory was the singer in the hottest band back then. Dallas' best friend was a gorgeous actor, named Griffin Harper, whom I dated briefly, though the relationship was doomed since he was obviously in love with Rory. The three of them were an incredible triaxial of talent. Tragically, Dallas was killed in a motorcycle accident when he was only twenty-three. I'd always wanted to have a group show with him, my photographs and his colorful, allegorical murals.

Standing on the corner of Queen and Spadina, I thought about August's gallery show in Ottawa. A wave of confusion swept over me, connecting my past in Toronto to my present in Watson. I felt like a fugitive. I needed to check in with my other life.

That night, I called Julie since I'd promised to help her out later in the week. Either she'd forgotten to turn her answering machine on or she was somewhere nearby and couldn't hear the phone. I called Christian.

"Hello," he answered, sounding out of breath.

"Hey, Christian."

"Anne?" he said, loudly. "Where the hell are you?"

"I'm in Toronto."

"Are you all right? What happened?"

"No. I'm fine." Something heavy collected in my chest.

I heard someone speaking in the background. The phone moved

away from Christian's mouth and I heard him say, "In Toronto. She's okay." He came back on the line. "We've been worried sick about you. What are you doing in Toronto?"

"I... needed some work done on my camera... and I figured I'd hang out for a day, go to a few galleries. That sort of thing." Each lie felt worse than the next. I'd once done it with ease. Now, it felt criminal.

"So you just took off without telling anyone?" Christian's voice moved up an octave. "How could you do that? You couldn't have left a note? Jesus!"

"I'm so sorry." My heart was beating in my throat.

"How'd you get there?" he asked.

"I took the bus."

"Took the bus," he echoed. "Mia and Julie have been sitting here wondering if they should call the police. I've been knocking on your door every hour. Finally had to let myself in to make sure you weren't lying on the floor in a coma."

"Oh my god," I whispered.

"And August and Brin have been driving around town, asking anyone if they'd seen you. August even called directory assistance and got the listings for every Hanes."

"Called where?" I said.

"Vancouver. He's been working his way down the list, calling complete strangers and asking if they have a daughter named, Anne. I'm... I'm at a loss for words here."

"Christian, I'm so, so sorry." I choked the words out. "I didn't mean to worry anyone."

"Well, at least we know you're all right." I heard a muffled knock on his end of the phone. "Yeah, come in," Christian yelled. "Hey, man. She's on the phone. She's okay." There was a pause and murmuring in the background. "Toronto," I heard Christian say. The phone rustled. "When are you coming back?"

"Tomorrow," I said.

There was a long pause. "Okay," Christian said. "We'll see you then." He hung up before I could say anything else.

I hung up the phone and did something I never do. I cried. I pictured Mia and Julie conferring about whether to call the police. I saw August driving around in his van, Brin riding shotgun, both of them scanning the streets. I saw August dialing the phone, questioning strangers. I saw Christian knocking on my door, the sound echoing in my empty studio.

A knot of guilt bloomed in my stomach. How could I have been so careless?

I went in the bathroom, washed my face in the sink, then looked in the mirror. A heart-shaped face, a heartless face. I closed my eyes, uncomfortable with myself.

The 6 a.m. bus carried me back the next morning, crawling mile by mile, while I tried to read a magazine. The restlessness I'd felt to leave two days before was now a restlessness to return.

It was still a hopeful and fresh morning when I climbed the stairs of The Factory at 7:30. A door opened just as I stepped on the second floor landing. Julie walked out of Christian's studio, followed by Christian. They were mid-sentence when they saw me.

Julie smiled her big smile and walked over to me. "Glad you're back," she said.

"Me too," I said, glancing at Christian. He stood in his doorway, doing up his jacket.

"Does she have all her arms and legs?" he said, concentrating on his buttons.

"Yes, Chris, she does," Julie said.

Christian walked to the top of the stairs. "Good," he said. He stopped in front of me, took my arms and pulled me into a crushing embrace. "Don't ever do that again," he said, quietly in my ear.

"I won't." I felt tears pressing behind my eyes. "I'm really, really sorry I worried you guys."

Christian released me and nodded. "Okay, Miss Julie, let's go eat." He turned to me. "You coming?"

I shook my head.

"Okay, let's go," Christian said, taking Julie by the arm.

I listened to their voices fading in the stairwell, then unlocked my door and went inside. When I closed the door, my four walls welcomed me home.

August was the one I was worried about. I knocked on his door a few hours later, then noticed the door to the darkroom was ajar.

He was pre-exposing some paper, bent over the counter, when I walked in.

"Hey," I said.

"Hey," he answered without turning around.

"Sorry for disappearing," I said. "I should have told someone I was going to Toronto."

August didn't respond. He continued to lay sheets of photo paper on top of the counter, the paper rustling like cardboard.

I watched his back, his hair sliding across his shoulders when he moved. He was wearing my favorite shirt, the denim one that was worn and soft looking.

A whole minute passed before he spoke.

"You have fun?"

"Yeah."

"Get your camera fixed?"

"No."

He turned around to get more paper from the shelf.

"Well, I'll let you get back to it," I said. I walked out the door and the air in the hallway was cool on my face. I was burning up.

I was already walking down the hallway when August called after me.

"Hey, Anne. If you need a camera, you can borrow mine."

"Thanks," I said.

I sat at my kitchen table, cool hands on my face. I felt unsteady, the motion of travel still in my blood. Arrival and departure were floating in the space between my two lives.

It felt like an era was ending. Just two days away from Watson and the axis had shifted. I wasn't ready for change yet, but it had already begun. What had been my temporary life was fading just when its permanence had begun to set in.

That night, I went through the photographs I'd taken over the last year in Watson. I was looking for stuff to send to Irene at *Exit*. There in front of me was the proof of my transitional life. I was wrong to think these pictures had no history. I had art photos of Mia, studies in movement and light. I had candid party shots of Christian and Julie. Some from the diner, of Mia and her boyfriend, Raymond. A whole slew I'd taken at The Underdog, some of the band, people dancing, Joe the bartender, blurred in motion behind the bar. I had shots of Caroline from her photo shoot and some of her from a party at Julie's. I had Brin and his girlfriend, Wendy, making a snowman behind The Factory last winter.

Something was missing.

I didn't have one photograph of August.

CHAPTER SEVEN

Redemption

A soft autumn rain was falling as Christian and I walked back from the diner. The air was sweet smelling, filling my lungs like pure oxygen. The wet streets shone like metal.

Pouring my coffee that morning at the diner, Mia had searched my face for changes. Toronto was only ninety miles away, but for those who never left Watson, it held a mysterious power, the ability to convert the innocent like a seductive cult. I smiled to reassure her that I was still Anne Hanes. And in Watson I still was.

Raindrops tapped the remaining leaves on the trees as we walked in silence up George Street. Christian was absorbed in something dreamy, his mouth in a half-smile.

I was thinking about photographing August.

It seemed obvious that I should have taken his picture by now. He'd been there when I'd photographed everyone else at parties. But he always managed to slide out of the shot at the last minute. In candid moments I'd pointed the camera at him. He always said, "Ah, you don't want to take my picture."

I had a creative itch to capture him on film. I imagined his face and got lost for a moment, remembering the way he looked at me when he asked if I was going to stay in Watson. Something squeezed in my chest and I had a sudden reflex to swallow.

"You okay?" Christian was looking at me. "Breakfast biting back?"

"No. Just thinking."

"About who?"

"August."

"Hmm…About his show in Ottawa? He'll be fine. Don't worry. It'll be good for him." Christian reached up and brushed a low hanging branch, scattering rain on our faces. "Despite what Caroline thinks," he added.

"Yeah, she asked me to butt out."

"Good idea. Don't mess with her. She has sharp teeth."

"And she uses them," I said under my breath.

I felt Christian's eyes on the side of my face. I kept walking, listening to the soft rain.

In front of The Factory, I waited while Christian hauled the garbage cans into the alley. A pale green Volvo was parked at the curb. It was a two-door sedan, probably ten years old. It made me think of my grandfather. He used to call that color "cream of green".

My grandfather was a painter. He painted cars. He's the reason I became a photographer.

His name was Abel Hannah and we moved into his house on Browning Avenue when I was three, after my grandmother died.

His specialty was oils. I associate that smell with my childhood and being in his attic studio. He began doing portraits after he retired from teaching at the Ontario College of Art. Everyone in the neighborhood had a Grampa Hannah original hanging in their living room.

After ten years of doing apple-cheeked kids and smiling grandparents, he got bored. His love of cars became his creative outlet. He'd always loved design and the way automobiles evolved over the years. The details thrilled him, the headlights, bumpers, side mirrors, hood ornaments, door handles.

"The colors," he used to say, as if red sedans and yellow convertibles

were thought up by some daring genius. He loved going to the car
dealership in our neighborhood and getting brochures of the lastest
models. The funny thing was, my grandfather wasn't the least bit
mechanically minded. He couldn't have cared less what was under
the hood of a car. It was the body that got his motor running.

Though he rarely drove, he owned several vintage cars, which
he polished and waxed every weekend. There was a 1970 red Cutlass
SS convertible, a 1956 two-tone Ford Fairlane, a 1947 Chevrolet
Fleetline in silver with dual exhaust, and a 1959 Cadillac Fleetwood
in aqua with fins on the back. The car he dreamed of owning was a
1967 Rolls Royce Silver Shadow with burgundy leather interior.

He started out painting portraits of his beloved fleet. After
he'd done several of each one, he started looking for cars in the
neighborhood. That's when he got into photography. He'd stroll up
and down the streets, snapping shots of cars he liked. Then he'd use
the photos as a reference for his portraits.

By the time I was thirteen, arthritis had moved into his hands. He
could still do the detail work, but needed to conserve the flexibility in
his fingers. That's when I learned to paint. He taught me how to hold
a brush to do the backgrounds, nothing too detailed, just large areas
of blue or ivory, maybe a few clouds or a tree. My career as an artist
was a short one. I wasn't very good at it.

When the arthritis moved into Grampa Hannah's knees, his photo
excursions were cut short. That's when I became a photographer. He'd
send me out with his camera in search of a certain car. My first
photos were horrible, out of focus, blurred, the cars cut in half.
Grampa was patient. He showed me how to take better pictures,
and then he showed me how to develop them.

I loved going out on Saturday afternoons with his old Leica
around my neck, stalking cars like a member of the paparazzi. I
started slipping in other photos, people mowing their lawns,
teenagers necking in alleyways, repeated shots of the boy who lived
a block over, who I had a mad crush on.

My shots of cars got better, but it was the ones of people that Grampa said showed promise.

By the time I was seventeen, Grampa was in a wheelchair and too old to paint. The photos of cars were no longer utilitarian references. They became the art. I became the art photographer. Along with my photos of people, he began framing my work. He hung them in his studio in between his car portraits.

My grandfather taught me the permanence of photography.

"The memory is subjective," he told me. "Looking back, you wonder if you remember things correctly. Details fade," he said in a cautioning voice, the way I'd heard people say, "beauty fades".

He believed in the 'objective eye', though not one devoid of emotion.

"To be a good documentalist, you must appreciate beauty. Showing someone a photograph of a flower is better than *telling* them what a flower looks like, because your heart is transmitted through your eye in a way your words can never translate."

He died in his sleep the year before my father. I was nineteen. He was eighty-four. I sometimes wonder what he would have thought about pornography. I've pictured it many times, him developing that picture, the *offensive* one. He would have commented on the details.

You see the curve of the young man's thigh? Your lighting is good. You gave the skin texture and proportion. Your sense of shadow gives the composition mystery.

Grampa Hannah believed in mystery. Unfortunately for me, when it came to my photograph, some people didn't. The piece of my heart transmitted through my eye, failed to evoke the beauty I had intended, for those who believed my vision was corrupt and my heart depraved.

As for the permanence of photography, I learned firsthand that it doesn't always survive the flames of judgement.

A few days after returning from Toronto, I run into August and Caroline in the park. I'm walking across the grass after snapping a few shots of a group of seniors doing t'ai chi by a massive maple tree, their slow, sweeping movements surrealistic under the autumn sun, when I see August and Caroline climbing up the bank from the beach, Maxine bounding ahead of them. Maxine sees me and stops, her ears curling forward. She recognizes me and starts running full speed in my direction. I swing my camera around to my back just in time. Maxine bounces to a stop at my feet, then leaps up, her paws hitting my chest, knocking me back a step.

"Max-ine!" Caroline yells from a distance.

August breaks into a run, getting to me in time to pull Maxine off before she's licked all of my face clean.

He wedges Maxine between his knees and looks at me. "She likes the way you taste, I guess."

"Just as long as she doesn't think I taste like dog food."

Maxine turns her head up to August and barks.

August nods at the strap across my chest. "You're shooting outside?"

"Yeah, I thought I'd try something different. I got some good ones of the t'ai chi-ers."

August leans towards me. "Hey, there's something I wanted to talk to you about," he says in a low voice.

"Yeah? What's that?"

"I'll talk to you later," he says. "You going to be around?"

"What are you two whispering about?" Caroline walks up behind August, then slips her arm through his and hugs him. She smiles her beautiful smile at me. "Sorry if Maxine is being overly friendly. She gets so excited when we go to the park. Doncha, beautiful girl?" Caroline bends over and Maxine squirms out from between August's legs, licking Caroline's mouth.

August reaches down and slaps Maxine's side. "I was just saying Maxine must like the way Anne tastes."

"Yeah, I don't need to exfoliate for awhile."

Caroline laughs. "You're funny," she says, eyeing me like she's just discovered something new about me.

"So you guys exploring the beach?" I say.

August perks up and reaches in the pocket of his jacket. He pulls out a small red brick. "Found this," he says, handing the brick to me.

The surface is rounded and feels like fine sandpaper. In the trough that runs down the middle is a round circle of blue glass, embedded in the red stone.

"Wow, beautiful," I say.

Caroline sighs and takes August's arm again, squeezing it. "One of these days, they're going to run out of bricks on the beach. You'll have to find something new to collect."

"I'll have to find a new beach or look further down river," August says.

Caroline looks at me and rolls her eyes, then looks at the side of August's face. "What am I going to do with you?"

August shrugs, then grins sheepishly. I watch his mouth, the way the corners tuck in and dimples pop out on his cheeks. He looks like a little boy, all sweetness and light. I keep studying his face, his high forehead and aquiline nose. Then I realize Caroline is watching me.

I smile at her to cover my embarrassment. "Hey, August," I say. "I'm putting together some stuff for my portfolio and I'd really like to do a portrait of you."

His eyes widen and he starts to smile.

"Good luck," Caroline says, squatting down to rub Maxine's belly. "August hates having his picture taken. If you want one of him, you'll have to take it when he's not looking."

August's eyes get distant, but he keeps the half smile on his face.

"Two years ago at my sister's wedding?" Caroline continues. "All the pictures came back and in every one, all you see is the back of his head."

"Oh," I say. "Well... it's not that big a —"

"Yeah, sure, I'll do it." August looks at me and nods.

Caroline stands up quickly and smoothes the creases out of her slacks. She stares at August for a moment, then laughs. "But you hate having your picture taken."

August puts his arm around Caroline's shoulder and pulls her against his side. "Well maybe it's time I got over it."

Caroline curls against August and puts her hand on his chest. "Really? That's wonderful, baby." She raises herself on tiptoes and kisses his cheek. Then she turns to me, smiling. "I want a copy so I can frame it."

"Sure. No problem," I say.

Later that evening, I come back from the diner and find Maxine sitting in front of August's door, staring intently up at the glass. When she sees me, she makes a timid whimpering noise in her throat. Then I notice the puddle of urine on the other side of the hallway in front of the door to the darkroom.

"Hey, Maxine," I whisper. "You get locked out?"

Her eyes follow me when I walk up to her and scratch her head. She doesn't jump up on me. Her tail is tucked in tight.

"It's okay," I whisper. "When you gotta go, you gotta go."

I listen for moment in front of the door. The glass is dark and it doesn't sound like anyone is home. I knock on the door and Maxine gets up and pushes against my leg.

After a moment, I knock again, and as soon as I do, a dark shape moves up to the glass and the door opens six inches.

"What is it?" Caroline says, her face poking out of the crack. The studio is dark behind her, and then I notice her shirt is unbuttoned. She's wearing a purple lacy bra.

"Ah, Maxine…" I start to say.

"What about her?" Caroline is staring at me.

"I guess she had to go." I motion down to my side.

Caroline looks at Maxine as if surprised to see her. "I told you to stay, Maxie. And be quiet."

Maxine makes a high-pitched whining noise in her throat.

"She had a little accident," I say, looking over my shoulder.

The door opens a few more inches. "Oh for Christ's sake, Maxie."

Maxine pushes in the door. Caroline sticks her leg out, blocking her way. "No, I told you to stay outside." Maxine whimpers as Caroline pushes her back out the door with her foot.

"I could take her to my studio," I say, taking Maxine by the collar.

"Thanks," Caroline whispers loudly and closes the door.

"Come on, Maxine. Looks like you're stuck with me."

Maxine looks at me, then at the closed door, then back at me. She lets out one loud bark, then follows me down the hall.

While Maxine drinks a bowl of water in my kitchen, I take a roll of paper towels down the hall and mop up the dog pee in front of the darkroom. When I get back, Maxine is curled up on my bed, her head between her paws.

She looks so sad. I lay on the bed and reach for a book. She curls up against my side.

A few minutes later, things get louder than normal next door.

At first it sounds like singing, a high breathy "ah – ah – ah". When the sound of creaking springs start, a steady rhythm that increases in speed, I jump off the bed and go into the kitchen.

For the next ten minutes, I talk out loud to Maxine, and keep moving until the singing and creaking stops next door. In the silence that follows, I realize I'm holding my breath.

A few minutes later, a pounding on the wall makes me jump.

"Maxee-een." Caroline yells through the wall. "Come on, sweetie. We're going home."

Maxine skids across the floor to the door.

I walk over and open it. Maxine tears out the door, her nails skittering across the hardwood in the hallway. I close the door and turn off the light.

I sit down at the kitchen table and put my face in my hands, my cheeks burning like I have a fever.

The next morning, while Christian and I are eating breakfast at the diner, August walks in and sits down on the stool beside me. Behind the counter, Mia smiles with surprise.

"What, d'you run out of toast and coffee at home?" Christian says.

"Yeah," August says. "Figured I'd join you guys. Can I have some eggs, Mia?"

Mia is staring at August. "Sure thing." She pours him some coffee, then says, "Hon, you have a boo-boo on your neck."

August's hand flies up to his neck, but before he covers it, I see the hickey, purple and striped, just below his earlobe.

Christian snaps his newspaper open. "Bit yourself shaving, eh?"

August ignores him and turns on his stool towards me. "So when do you want to do this portrait thing? I'm not doing anything this afternoon."

I glance at the hickey. "Ah, yeah, sure. How 'bout after breakfast?"

August nods.

I blow air out between my lips. "So what did you want to talk to me about?"

Christian clears his throat and continues reading the newspaper. "Talk louder. I can't hear you guys."

August laughs. He leans over to me and rests his elbows on the counter. The clean smell of laundry detergent rises from his demin shirt. "About my show in Ottawa."

"You're doing it for sure?"

August grins and bumps me with his shoulder. "Yeah, I'm doing it. I just wondered… you've been to those kind of things, right?" I nod. "Do I have to wear a suit? And are they going to expect me to answer a lot of questions, or do I just stand there and try and look intelligent?"

His hand is resting beside my coffee cup, the skin on the back, dark and soft. I reach out and give his fingers a squeeze.

"You can wear whatever you want. You're the artist."

August looks straight ahead and I see a smile starting to form. Then he drops his head quickly. "Jeez, I can't believe I'm doing this."

Christian wipes his mouth with a napkin, tucks some bills under the coffee cup and slides off his stool. "Get used to it, buddy. This is the shape of future things to come."

"Where do you want me?" August says, standing in the middle of my kitchen.

Now that we're back at my studio, I'm nervous about photographing him.

"By the window."

He swivels around, his arms jerking at his sides.

I grab a few rolls of black and white from the fridge. "Can I ask you something?"

August turns around.

"What made you change your mind about having your photograph taken?"

August looks away, pinching the web of his hand with his thumb and forefinger. He shrugs. "'Cause it's important to you. And you're good at it. This is what you do."

I see his eyes open up and color warm his face. He trusts me with his image. I pray my hesitating finger doesn't come out of hiding.

"Too much light," I say, walking over to him.

After drawing the large canvas curtain across the window, I set up an umbrella light, turn on the overhead light and the floor lamp behind me. The room expands with a warm white glow.

"Can I ask you something else?"

"Sure," August says, picking up my tripod and adjusting the legs.

"How come you don't shoot people?"

August sets the tripod on the floor, unscrews the arm, then tightens it in position. He laughs and brushes his hair back. "I wasn't very good at getting people to pose for me."

"Seriously?"

August's eyes get a faraway look. "Yeah, I had a reputation for being a pest."

When August was thirteen, the Curve Lake Band Council and the government decided they needed some documentation of life on the reserve. Funds were supplied to buy a camera. It sat in the board room of the council house for six months. No one came forward with any interest in taking pictures. August was curious and stole the camera. No one noticed. He was a teenager, restless and bored, hoping to get into some mischief. Instead, he got interested in photography. He learned by trial and error. When he got frustrated with taking bad pictures, the band council, who by now thought they had their photographer, went in search of someone to show August how to use the camera. They found a man by the name of Jeroen Slatterly, a newspaper photographer for the Toronto Star, who was also keenly interested in aboriginal culture.

Jeroen Slatterly came up to the reservation for what was supposed to be a week. He ended up staying a month, and later published a photo essay book on Curve Lake. He taught August the fundamentals of photography, and when he saw how interested August was in the process, he mentored him in becoming a photographer.

Confident he knew what he was doing, August set about documenting life on the reservation. Only problem was, nobody particularly liked having their picture taken. At first, they begrudgingly let August shoot them at work, or hanging out. Then they started dodging him when they saw him coming with his camera. Finally, they started telling him to get lost.

"I was a bit obsessed," August says. "I'd shoot everything and anyone. Boy, the women… they were the worst. If I shot them with curlers in their hair or wearing their laundry-day clothes, they got violent. Had a flower pot thrown at me once." August smiles, but it fades quickly. "I guess they didn't want to see what they'd looked like a few years later when the pictures would still be there. Maybe they thought it wrecked the future when there was too much of the past hanging around." He shrugs and pinches the web of his hand. "Don't know... It wasn't much later that I moved to town. Worked at I.G.A., then at the diner. Didn't take my camera out for three years. Then one day I saw the most amazing pine tree down by the river." He pauses and looks at me. "It didn't seem to mind when I took its picture."

While August was talking, I set up my camera, and now I have him nicely framed in the viewfinder. He has that natural grace and beauty, like Mia. Something a little God-like about their presence. There's just one problem. Something about his shirt is bugging me. The pearl snaps down the front are reflecting little flares of light.

"Can you turn to your left a bit?"

August moves left, but the glare is still there. I have him turn right, angle his body, but the damn buttons are still flashing or August ends up turned sideways to the camera and I definitely want to shoot him full on.

He sees me staring and looks at the front of his shirt. "Is this the problem?" he says.

"Yeah."

In one movement, he rips the snaps open and slips the shirt off. No modesty at all. Heat crawls up my face. The way his black hair contrasts with his brown skin is sublime. His chest is only slightly curved with muscle, his nipples, copper-colored, and he has no body hair. His stomach is flat, not rippled, and a band of paler skin runs just above the waistband of his jeans.

I can't believe how beautiful he is.

He looks up at me, his eyes willing, so natural and trusting, no posing or self-consciousness. I'm going to have a hard time shooting objectively. There's just one more small problem. The hickey. It mars the smoothness of his skin, and will come out as a dark blotch in black and white.

I walk up to him and stop. "Can I?" I pull some of his hair foreward.

August stands very still, looking straight ahead. I move back. It's still visible. I adjust his hair again, trying to figure out if he looks better with it falling over his shoulders or swept back. I can always put some makeup on the hickey. August senses me trying to decide and gathers up his hair and pulls it into a pony tail. I shake my head. He lets it fall over his shoulders again.

Standing close to him, I can feel the heat radiating off his chest and smell his warm clean scent. I close my eyes to refocus. I need to get a mental image in my mind of how the photograph will look.

When I open my eyes again, August's face has moved close to mine, his features blurred. Before I can move back, he does the most surprising thing. He leans forward and kisses me on the lips. Then he takes my face in his hands and does it again, slower this time, taking my bottom lip into his mouth, curiously, taking his time. The room spins around me and blood pounds in my ears.

August pulls his head back and looks at me. I stand there for a moment with my mouth hanging open. Then my thoughts collect all at once.

"Why did you do that?"

August has this expression on his face, like he just opened a door and realized he's in the wrong room. "Don't know. I thought you wanted me to."

"No-o." I hate the way my voice gets high and uncertain. I move a safe distance away and stand behind the tripod. "No," I say again. "You can't just... you're not suppose..."

"Stop freaking out." August looks uncomfortable now. "It's not a big deal."

I take a breath and hold it in, then release it. "You're right. Not a big deal. Forget it."

My hands fumble with the camera. When I look through the

viewfinder, August's head is turned to the side and his cheek is gathered in thought.

Awkwardness fills the room.

"This is going to look great," I say, forcing enthusiasm into my voice.

"Yeah?" August sounds half-hearted.

Just then the cukoo clock next door bongs the hour. The little bird begins to chirp.

August turns his head and looks past me, his face surprised. "I've never heard what that sounds like in here," he says. He frowns. "I hope it's not annoying."

"No," I say. "I hardly notice it anymore."

August shakes his head, grinning. "I've had that clock so long, I don't think I could live without it."

The moment of awkwardness has passed. It's as if the kiss never happened. *It never happened*, I repeat to myself. His hands didn't cup my face with such tenderness I wanted to cry, and his lips didn't touch mine with an electricity that stirred every nerve in my body.

"Where did you get the clock?" I ask.

"It was my grandmother's. She had lots of clocks, but that one was her favorite."

"Did she collect them?"

August laughs. "Yeah, sort of. I think she was trying to get me more comfortable with the concept of time."

"You had problems telling time?"

August raises his eyebrows. "Yeah, you could say that. My grandmother thought I had a problem with the future."

...*like holding back the future*. That's what August had said about photography.

"What kind of problem?" I lean down to look at August through the viewfinder. His hair has fallen over his shoulders and for some reason, the hickey is now invisible. I snap a test shot.

August is lost in thought and doesn't seem to notice.

"She said, 'you have the spirit of the future sitting on your shoulder. Problem is, you don't *want* the future. You want to stop time.'" August shrugs and looks to the side, tracing his palm with his index finger. I snap another shot. "It's easy to know who you are in the present, but it's hard to look at yourself before and after."

I look up over the camera. "Wow. That's true isn't it?"

August smiles with one side of his mouth. "Yeah. Just 'cause you can see the future, doesn't always mean you can change it."

I look in the viewfinder, but my vision is unfocused. I've just realized something fundamental about August. He *can* see the future. I've seen him predict things that haven't happened yet – the time Christian got fired from a job, Mia got a ten dollar tip, Julie broke up with the jerk lawyer she was dating last year.

"Tell me more about your Grandmother," I say.

August shifts his weight to one leg. Against the off-white canvas backdrop, his skin has depth. His black hair has a blue halo around it. When the moment comes, I know it's going to be a once in a lifetime photograph.

"Well..." he says and begins telling the story.

Before August learned how to tell time, it was a concept he thought existed inside himself, a personal chronology that he controlled. Lacking parental discipline or responsibility, he came and went as he pleased. By the age of ten, after living with various aunts and uncles, he'd become hard to handle and his grandmother stepped in and enforced some rules. That's when August became aware of clocks. If he came home late, she'd look at her wristwatch and scold him. If he overstayed his welcome at someone's house, they'd look at the clock and tell him it was 'time' to go home. He became aware of a different kind of time, the kind that existed outside of himself, one he could see and hear.

It was people's relationships with their clocks that began to fascinate him. His Uncle Dale's pride in his oak grandfather clock, which he wound faithfully once a week. His cousin Sally's Timex wristwatch with the glowing hands, a birthday present she proudly showed everyone, and when August slept over, they'd hide under the blankets and watch it glow on their pajamas. His cousin Bert's Mickey Mouse alarm clock, with bell-ears on top and Mickey's hands inching around the numbers. His Uncle Steve had a pocket watch that had belonged to his grandfather, and it hung on a gold chain from his vest pocket, and when he popped the lid open to read the time, his posture got straighter and he held his head higher.

August's grandmother received the cuckoo clock from her husband, a gift he brought all the way back from Sudbury, the nickel mining town in Northern Ontario. He wanted her to have a clock that rang, so she could count the hours until he returned from his next trip to the nickel mines. Only, he didn't realize that after his death, whenever the tiny doors opened up and the little bird came out, it made her count the hours of an absence from which he'd never return. She told August the little bird was in mourning and had to cry every hour for eternity.

August pauses in his story. I've snapped a few shots of him, some with his face animated, some with wistful expressions.

He sighs now, as though impatient.

"It started bugging me that people were so controlled by their clocks. My grandmother's sadness when my grandfather died. Other people were impatient if time was dragging, or irritated if it was moving too fast for them to do everything they needed to do. They were pressured by deadlines, or enforcing curfews."

August, by then an unruly teenager, began breaking curfews and coming home late for dinner. It seemed to him, whenever his grandmother looked at the clock or her wristwatch, he got into trouble with her. The idea of stopping time began to take hold.

While she slept one night, August took her alarm clock out of her bedroom and removed the batteries. He took her wristwatch off the night stand and hid it. Her clock radio above the sink got unplugged. A few other table clocks got gum shoved inside to stop the cogs from turning. The cuckoo clock got wedged with gum as well.

The next morning when his grandmother got up at her usual time, she didn't say anything. August hung around the house all day, pretending to be absorbed in cutting photographs out of an old issue of Mclean's magazine. He watched her, waiting for her to check the time. She didn't look at a clock all day. She cooked, cleaned, read as if she had all the time in the world.

Finally, August couldn't stand it any longer and said, "Hey, Gramma, what time is it?"

She looked at him calmly and said, "I wouldn't know. It looks like time has stopped."

Her words made August shiver, as if he'd somehow stopped all the clocks in the world and time had ceased to exist. He was scared, his game suddenly not funny anymore. His grandmother sighed and motioned him over to her. She took his hands and stroked the backs of them.

"Don't be afraid of the future, August," she said. "It's waiting to welcome you. Sitting on your shoulder like the messenger eagle. Time isn't your enemy. Your fear of it is."

August held onto her words, trying to draw comfort from them, but a part of him was still afraid that time would try and take his joy.

August's eyes look directly into the camera, full of love and sadness. "When my grandmother died," he says, "I went to her house and stopped all the clocks again. I didn't want her to go. I went to get the cuckoo clock down off the wall, and as soon as I had it in my hands, the hour stuck three and that stupid little bird came out of its house and pecked me on the forehead."

August looks at the camera and laughs. Then his eyes move off to the side, the smile on his mouth folding and unfolding. Then I see the tear, in his left eye, welling up, quivering for a moment, trying to hang on. It falls down his cheek slowly. His mouth is tucked in, a wistful smile, nostalgic, sad and happy, the face of a clown.

The moment has come, powerful and committed. I snap three shots in a row, unconscious flicks of my finger, as if someone else is controlling me, telling me I need to capture this picture.

It's only when my head starts buzzing and my vision blurs that I realize how long I've been holding my breath. I let it out and look at August over the top of the camera.

He grins sheepishly, tilting his head. "I know. Silly story."

I start to speak, then have to clear my throat. "I thought it was beautiful."

August straightens up. "Yeah?"

"I wish I could have met her."

August starts nodding and looks at me seriously. "I wish you could have met her, too."

I usually wait a while to develop film I've just shot. I have this weird idea that the images need to set on the film before they become permenant. But right now, I'm anxious to develop the film of August.

"So we're done?" August says.

"Yeah, I got the one."

"Want me to help in the darkroom?" he says.

"No, I should do these alone. Can't work with you there. You're the subject."

August presses his lips together, then nods. "Okay then."

After he's gone, I sit down on the edge of the bed and lay my hand over my chest, feeling the thumping of my heart against my fingers. Each time I imagine August's face, ripples of goose bumps shoot up my arms and across my shoulders. I haven't felt this kind of exhilaration in a long time. I felt it after taking the photograph of Eric and Daniel, before everything beautiful got painted with accusations and ugliness.

It's only now that I realize I've been waiting to prove myself again, to wipe sin from my reputation and redeem myself. In trusting me, August has given me my redemption.

In the darkroom, I develop the first few shots. They're good, but I can see the moment isn't there yet. It's in progress, building like seismic pressure, waiting out time until everything aligns.

The last three shots emerge in the developing trays, August's image surfacing from the depths of the paper, shadows darkening, his face getting sharper, and then the full image is there. I hang the three photos up, decide on the second one immediately, then stare at the wall as they dry, waiting for my objectivity to return.

Later I take the best shot back to my studio, make a pot of coffee, then sit on the bed with the photo between my hands. It's so powerful, it's hard to look at, harder to look away. His face is naked, trusting the camera. There's the paradox of his expression, a tear and a smile, his moment of stillness after the story.

Then it hits me. As I stare at his frozen image, I realize I've stopped time. I captured a fragment of the story, a moment that defines August.

The emotions in the photograph sum up who he is, grief and joy, two ends of the spectrum.

I stare at his body, his black hair falling over his shoulders, his melancholy blue eyes, his velvet face. There is nothing invented about him. He is real. Beautiful and soulful.

I'm going to call the photograph, Soul Of A Man.

CHAPTER EIGHT

Hands of Doom

Christian's fingers are lined with orange dust as he sands rust off a steel beam, a trick of the light altering his skin to tendon and bone, half revealed like a chiaroscuro painting. He works the sandpaper back and forth, leaning his whole body into it, the strength in his arms feeding confidence into his hands.

Christian has large hands that look like they could cure anything. Unfortunately, he doesn't think so. He works them hard, welding, sanding, hammering, as though he's punishing them, brutalizing them with labor, making them ugly so he can justify the cruelty he thinks is in his touch.

We're in the parking lot behind The Factory on a deathly quiet Tuesday afternoon. I'm watching Christian finish a new sculpture for the Turkey Fest party in two weeks. It's a huge bow and arrow, like the one the aboriginals used to hunt turkeys, he says. He's going to call it *Victory*.

He doesn't talk as he works, and I'm content just to watch his hands being creative. He doesn't see how they become completely intimate with the steel. Christian has intimacy issues.

Four years ago, Christian met a woman at The Underdog. She was a teacher, wild and voluptuous, ten years older than Christian. Neither of them was looking for more than a night of guilt-free sex.

Back at her place, well into their foreplay, Christian was absorbed in fondling her creamy breasts, when his thumb rubbed over a large, hard lump.

"What's this?" he asked, rubbing his thumb over the lump again.

"Hmm, that's good," the woman murmured, covering Christian's hand with her own and pressing harder.

She noticed his attention had turned from sensual to scientific. Christian took her hand and guided her fingers to the lump.

She sat up, swallowing hard, her breath rushed. "Oh God," she whispered.

Christian took her to the emergency room that night. Then he took her home after the doctor ordered a mammogram and a needle biopsy for the next day. She was white-faced and silent. Christian was horrified. His hands had become divining rods for a future he would not have a part in. How was he supposed to act with a stranger whose beautiful breasts he had hours earlier lusted after, and was now sharing a sickening discovery with? He didn't know her well enough to comfort her. And seeing her naked didn't come anywhere close to the privacy he was now invading.

He didn't hear from her for several weeks, and was trying hard to forget the incident. Then he ran into her on the street, coming out of the drugstore. She looked gray and drawn, her wild voluptuousness withered.

It was cancer, she told him. They'd do a mastectomy, but it didn't look good. They'd found another lump in the lymph node under her arm, indicating it had spread. She was right. Six months later, she died.

When Christian told me the story, he referred to his "hands of doom". I remember him holding his hands up and turning his palms towards me.

"Midas had the golden touch," he said. "I have the cancerous touch."

It's amazing the things we come up with to torture ourselves.

"I'm definitely not a breast man anymore," Christian said.

Christian stops sanding and straightens up, holding his lower back with both hands. He wipes his brow on his sleeve and looks up at the late afternoon sun.

"Time for a beer," he says.

"You've earned it," I say.

He smiles and looks at me for a moment, then closes his eyes and sucks in a loud breath. "Haven't seen Nature Boy around much."

I look at the metal fire escape that leads up to the second floor of The Factory. From down here, the big window in my studio mirrors the waving pine trees and patches of blue sky.

"He's working on last minute stuff for his show," I say.

"He's going to be back in time for the party, right?"

"He gets back the day before. Don't worry."

Christian walks over to where I'm sitting on the low stone wall that separates our parking lot from the one next door. He stops in front of me, rubbing dust off his palms on the front of his jeans.

I reach over and take hold of his hands.

"Good hands," I say, rubbing my thumbs in the divots of his palms. "Hands of doom don't make art like that. You're cured."

Christian lets out a laugh. "It's that easy, huh?"

I let go of his hands and stand up. "It's that easy."

Hands of doom. Healing hands. The hand of God. The hands of time.

August's hands.

When he took my face in his hands, it was more intimate than his kiss. The way he held me, his fingers on my temples, like his discovery of tenderness was new.

I let him touch me.

He's touched me.

September comes to an end in a swirl of colored leaves and frost-edged mornings. Every day I take the photo of August out of my filing cabinet and look at it. He hasn't asked about it, and I'm afraid to show it to him. I'm afraid he will see my heart transmitted through my eye. I'm also aware of an encroaching feeling of separation. The photograph is like a new passport, giving me permission to travel again.

Finally, I show it to Mia.

"Wow, that's really good," she says. "He looks so innocent," she adds, softly.

"I think it may be the best photograph I've ever taken," I say.

She looks at me, and then at the photograph, holding it delicately between her fingers like it's a fragile document.

"What are you going to do with it?"

"I don't know," I say.

Her head snaps up. "You have to send it out. If you think this is the best thing you've ever done, people should see it."

I do something that surprises me. I hug Mia, long and tight.

She squirms in my arms. "I hope this doesn't mean you're replacing me with August as your favorite model."

I hug her tighter then release her. "No. I think that was a one shot deal."

The next day, I mail Soul Of A Man off to my friend, Irene, at Exit magazine. After I drop the envelope in the mailbox, I stand holding the chute open, knowing that as soon as I let the door close, I have committed to being Albertine Hannah again.

The Friday night before August leaves for Ottawa, Caroline comes over to his studio for their weekly dinner.

I'd seen them earlier in the day at I.G.A. They were standing in the gourmet food aisle, their heads touching as they read the ingredients on a bottle of sun-dried tomatoes. I watched from behind my shopping cart in Dairy as Caroline looked up into August's face, and then tucked a lock of his hair behind his ear. August was still absorbed in reading the label on the bottle. Caroline gazed at his face with the look of a new lover who is searching for the essence that makes them quiver and holds their heart in a prison they are powerless to escape. August looked up and caught her expression. He put his arm around her, pulling her into his safe harbor, kissing the crease of apprehension on her forehead. She laid her head on his shoulder and together they pushed their cart, unhurried, down the aisle.

Later on, I toss a TV dinner in the microwave and sit down at the table to read a magazine, distracting myself with colorful pictures of the rich and beautiful.

Next door, Caroline and August are cooking, their voices animated, Van Morrison on the CD player.

I'm trying not to listen, but after half an hour, I start humming along with their stereo.

Then suddenly the music stops.

I hear Caroline, her voice rising and falling, getting louder until her words are audible.

"But you said you hadn't decided if you were going."

August's reply is a low murmur.

"I can't believe you didn't discuss this with me," Caroline says. There's a moment of silence, then, "So you're going. Unbelievable."

August says something.

"Yeah?" Caroline says, her voice rising. "I'll bet I know who helped you decide."

"Keep your voice down," August says.

"I could care less if she hears me."

There's a moment of dead silence. Then something shatters on the floor, an explosive tinkling of glass.

"What the hell are you doing?" August's voice is high-pitched with disbelief.

Something thumps on the floor, a scuffle, rubber-soled shoes squeaking, then August's voice saying loudly, "don't."

There's a beat of nothing, then the staccato of high heels across the floor.

The slap is so loud, I step back and touch my face.

I hear Caroline gasp. "I'm sorry, baby. I'm sorry. Let me kiss it better."

There's another scuffle of feet, the door opening, then slamming hard enough, the glass pane rattles. August's feet descend the stairs in a heavy cascade of thuds. The front door of the building slams, echoing up the stairwell like a cannon shot.

I'm standing in the middle of the kitchen, holding in a painful breath.

I hear August's door open, footsteps in the hall, then a sharp volley of raps on my door.

"Anne? I know you're in there. Anne? Open the door. I want to talk to you."

I stand frozen, my heart pounding in my ears.

"Anne. God dammit! I know you're there."

She pounds on the door with her fist, her shadow moving behind the glass.

I hold my breath, counting silently, one, two, three, four, five...

She pounds once more on the door and I jump, losing count. Her shadow retreats and her staccato footsteps fade down the hall.

I sit down in a chair, my knees trembling.

October fourth, the day August leaves to go to Ottawa, there is one last wave of Indian summer. By noon, the temperature climbs to seventy degrees and people are outside in short sleeves, smiling at the sun as if she has thrown a party.

The night before, August asked me to drive him to the train station.

"Caroline's doing a wedding in Ennismore," he said.

I hesitated.

"And Christian's working that day," he added.

"Sure," I said.

"I really appreciate it," August said, his blue eyes pure and undamaged, showing no trace of the slap.

The morning he leaves, he's nervous and fidgety. I stand in the doorway of his studio, waiting, while he looks around, patting the breast pockets of his jean jacket.

"You can use my van while I'm away," he says.

"Thanks."

"Can you water my plants? Damn, I forgot to clean out the fridge."

"I'll do it."

"And can you take my mail in? And tell Christian if he wants to borrow my electric screwdriver he has to recharge it. He always forgets to do that."

"Stop worrying."

August looks away. "I'm not worrying," he says, quietly.

"We'd better go."

August picks up his knapsack and looks around one last time, as if he's leaving for good.

He releases a breath. "Okay. Ready."

When we're walking out of the station after getting August's ticket, he says, "I've only been to Ottawa once. Hope I don't get lost."

"Leave a bread crumb trail wherever you go."

August looks at me, his face serious, then his expression dissolves and he smiles, running his hands through his hair. "Christ, I'm a mess."

I squeeze his arm and feel how wrong he is, his flesh and bones solid under my fingers.

The Watson Train Depot hasn't moved into this century yet. It still has an old wooden platform outside, a convex awning overhead with a suspended clock, old metal baggage trolleys and wood benches worn smooth and pearly gray. August and I stand on the edge of the platform looking at the weeds growing up out of the gravel inside the tracks. There are only two other people waiting to take the train. A few more are waiting for people to arrive. The wind is wild and hot, blowing black-rimmed clouds across the sun. Our shadows are long black ribbons, stretching out unbroken on the platform, as though the sun and wind have given us permission to be larger than life today.

August's shadow moves across mine. I look up and he's staring at me, chewing the inside of his cheek like he's working up to saying something.

Suddenly the wind stops and the clouds uncover the sun.

Down the tracks I hear the train, a distant rattle, rolling closer.

August jerks his head towards the station building. "You want to go buy a ticket and come with me?"

I open my mouth to speak. I want to. I really want to.

"Forget it. Dumb idea." August shakes his head and looks at his watch. He pushes his sleeve down and studies the button on his cuff. "You're a big part of me doing this. I wish you could be there for my opening." He turns his head away from me and says quickly, "I'll miss you."

His words are almost drowned out by the train as it moves past us, brakes hissing, engines rocking. I can't take my eyes off August. I'm suddenly afraid I'll never see him again.

"Okay. Bye," he says. He doesn't move.

"Bye," I say.

August frowns and then his face goes soft and tender.

I blink and my vision blurs. I'm afraid I'm really going to start crying, and I swallow over and over again, trying to push it back inside.

August puts his hands on my arms and pulls me towards him. He hugs me, gently at first, then harder, his nose against the softest part of my neck, his breath damp on my skin. Then he releases me and cups my face in his hands, just like he did the afternoon I took his photograph.

I start to say his name, but he kisses me, quickly. Then he seems to change his mind, his hands pulling my face back to him and this time he really kisses me. And keeps on kissing me.

I swear to God I've never been kissed like this before. Time stops. I spin in place. I ache for August, feeling his fingers on my temples.

"All aboard!"

We pull apart.

August is wide-eyed. "I didn't mean to do that," he says.

"Me neither."

"I'd better go," August says. He turns and jumps on the train.

I stand looking up at him, still back in the moment when his tongue touched the inside of my lip and made me quiver.

The train releases a hissing sigh and lurches forward.

August is standing in the doorway, the surprised look still on his face, his smile wavering, and as the train pulls away, he raises his hand and gives me a small wave.

I start smiling so hard, my face hurts. I raise my arm and wave.

The last sight I have of August, he is grinning, his teeth glinting in the sun.

I watch the train disappear down the tracks, the last car fishtailing out of sight. When I turn to leave, a young woman is facing me, further down the platform, a puzzled expression on her face. An older woman is beside her, bending down to retrieve a shoulder bag from the platform.

I walk towards the door to the station, watching the young woman, wondering why she is still staring at me.

Just before I reach the door, I see her more clearly. Her face has turned into a scowl, her eyes full of disgust.

I walk into the station, shivering when the cold, dry air envelops me. Then I remember where I know the young woman from. She works for Caroline.

I drive August's van to the diner, torn between guilt and giddiness. It's ten after two. Mia's shift ends at two-thirty.

When I walk in, she smiles and waves, and pours me a cup of coffee at the counter.

"Where you coming from all happy?" she says.

"Train station." I sit on a stool.

"Oh," Mia says, drawing the word out. "He get off alright?"

I nod. I can't control my mouth. A grin flicks across my lips, and I bite the insides of my cheeks to get rid of it.

Mia is holding the pot of coffee, watching me.

"What?" I say.

"You kissed him, didn't you?"

"Jesus."

"You have that goofy look on your face, and your lipstick's all smeared."

I wipe my mouth, and take a sip of coffee. It's bitter and burnt-tasting.

"Sorry. It's not a fresh pot," Mia says, taking the cup from me. "I get off in a minute. You want to go get coffee somewhere else?"

"Sure," I say.

I drive August's van up George Street with the windows rolled down, a hot earthy smell on the wind.

"I've been thinking about that picture," Mia says, leaning her head out the passenger side window.

"Yeah?"

"There's a reason it's so good," she says.

"Why's that?"

"Because you love August."

"Wow. What?"

Mia presses her lips into a thin line. "I just don't know if it's the smartest thing to be doing. You don't know what you're up against."

Mia sits on my bed while I try to find some clean cups for coffee. The counter is littered with dirty dishes. I fish two cups out of the mess and start washing them.

Mia gets up and comes into the kitchen, taking the clean cups from me and drying them on a dishtowel.

"So, you're not denying it."

"Denying what?"

"August."

I pour water in the coffeemaker. "August is involved with someone."

Mia snorts. "Caroline? We know what that's all about."

I turn to her. "We do?"

Mia pauses, her eyes searching my face. Then she looks away and starts putting dishes in the sink. She turns on the tap and squirts some soap in the water. We both watch the soap mushroom up in the sink. I reach over and turn the tap off before the foam overtakes the counter top.

Mia pushes back her sleeves and plunges her hands in the soapy water. Then she just leaves them there.

"Caroline dated Raymond's younger brother in high school," she says. "Billy bought her diamond earrings. In *high school*. If she caught someone staring at her ears, she'd say 'yes, they're real'. But when Billy wouldn't sleep with her..." Mia shakes her head and begins washing the dishes. "She pushed him till she got her way."

Mia starts scrubbing a pot I made Kraft Dinner in four days ago. "This is going to sound weird, but Billy wanted to save himself for marriage. He was really religious, *is* really religious. So Caroline waited till one weekend when her parents were out of town. She made dinner for him, nicked a bottle of wine from the wine cellar, got him drunk. Then she tied him to her bed with bungee cords. Four-poster with a canopy."

Mia scrubs the pot in an angry rhythm. "He was seventeen. Guys that age are horny all the time. She just sat on him and went to town. Billy tried to fight it, but... After, he started crying. She slapped him so hard he had a handprint on his face for a week. Billy didn't want anything to do with her after that. But when he wouldn't return her phone calls and kept avoiding her at school, she started a rumor that Billy had gotten her pregnant and forced her to have an abortion. She made sure everyone saw her crying with her girlfriends."

Mia gives up on the pot and throws it back in the sink. "You really ought to presoak."

"What happened to Billy?"

Mia closes her eyes. "Two weeks later, he tried to slash his wrists."

"Jesus."

Mia looks at me. "He couldn't get a date for the rest of high school. Girls avoided him like the plague. The principal got wind of the rumor and hauled him into the office and lectured him on the responsibilities of teenage sex. Billy was too embarrassed to tell anyone except Raymond what really happened. He's nearly thirty and he's still afraid of women."

Mia sits down at the table and turns sideways in the chair. She crosses her legs and picks at a pill on her white stockings. "I have never told anyone about this. The only reason I can stand to look at her is because of August."

Neither of us says anything for a moment. The coffeemaker gurgles.

"She hits him," I say.

Mia opens her mouth, then closes it and shakes her head. "Dammit, I knew it. I hoped it was different with him." Mia looks at me. "How do you know?"

"I've heard them." I nod towards my bedroom wall.

"Jesus." Mia stares at me. "With her it's all about control. I think she gets off on hurting people."

"August puts up with it."

"'Cause he thinks he's supposed to."

"He's not that dumb."

"It's not stupidity," Mia says. "If you were raised the way he was, passed around from family to family. He just wants to be loved."

Watson becomes a different place in August's absence. A fierce northern wind blows through two days after he leaves and strips the trees bare. The afternoon sun comes in my window, golden and brief, and the night falls swiftly, the streets tunnels of damp and quiet dark. My floor is cold in the mornings and on the fourth day, the ancient radiator clangs to life, filling my studio with swampy-smelling heat.

Fall brings a reel of memories of Toronto. Queen Street lit with blue light, people hurrying into restaurants while dry leaves blow through the empty patios out front. The city regains its hum, freed from the oppressive heat and humidity of summer, and at twilight it is at its best, glowing with energy, the cold air quickening, waiting for the darkness to descend and the nightlife to begin.

I miss those moments, being surrounded by Toronto people.

Five days after August leaves, I remember I was supposed to clean out his fridge. His studio is stuffy with heat and unmoved air. It's more than quiet in his kitchen, there is a stillness, as if the world has continued to spin outside his walls, while inside, time has stopped. Then I realize why. The cuckoo clock isn't ticking. I walk over and look up at it. The hands are stopped at ten after five. The tiny wood doors that house the chirping bird are closed tight. Closed for business. No one's home.

The stillness is profound. No trace of life. Dust has collected. Chairs are unmoved. August's essence is missing.

That night, I dream that August is an astronaut. He's floating in space, in a huge white suit, tethered to his space ship by a long rope. His arms are spread, his legs crossed, and inside his visor, his eyes are closed in sleep. He rocks and tilts like a boat moored to a dock, while stars bob in the endless black around him. Then Caroline appears outside the ship. She reaches over and undoes August's lifeline. His eyes open, but his arms and legs don't move out of their pose. As he drifts away, he smiles, and when he's almost a speck in black space, he gives a small wave, just like he did at the train station.

I wake up feeling helpless to pull him back to the safety of earth.

The morning August is due back from Ottawa, I realize I don't know if he's arranged for anyone to pick him up at the train station. I debate for a whole hour whether I should go. I have his van, therefore, he may assume I'm picking him up. But, I don't want to be presumptuous. He would have called if he wanted me to pick him up. But if I don't go, he may be standing there waiting. God, I hate this. I'm dying to see him. I wonder if he remembers that kiss. I wish I could stop thinking about it.

I wait till the last minute, then jump in the van and drive like mad to get there.

When I return from the train station twenty-five minutes later, I can't believe how stupid I am.

Caroline was there ahead of me. I walked out on the platform in time to see August stepping off the train and into the waiting arms of Caroline. She clung to him and kissed him deeply, their embrace lengthening, going on long enough for me to watch, white-faced, my insides collapsing as if I'd been punched. I slipped away and went back to the van, unsure whether to leave it and walk home, or wait and give August the keys.

Then I saw them, coming across the parking lot arm in arm. When August saw me, he smiled and waved before his expression faltered, and he dropped his arm and looked quickly at Caroline. She was staring at me calmly.

"Hi," I said. "Didn't know if anyone was picking August up."

"I've got my car," Caroline said.

"Okay, well, just thought I'd check," I said.

August cleared his throat and started to speak. "Thanks. Are you –"

Caroline cut him off. "Thanks, Anne. We'll see you later."

I watched them walk away. August looked over his shoulder once, his expression unreadable.

Later that night, I wake up feeling cold air on my face. When I look across the room, I think I see my door closing and hear soft footsteps in the hall.

When I get up the next morning there is a small brown box on my kitchen table. Inside is a pair of salt and pepper shakers shaped like little cameras, one black, one white.

Christian's Thanksgiving party is tonight. He and Julie have been decorating all weekend. Everyone is supposed to bring something made with turkey. I'm doing a turkey salad, using leftovers Mia got from the diner.

When I come back from buying salad stuff at the store, I notice the red light is on above the darkroom door. When I get to the top of the stairs, the light goes off and the door opens. August steps out in the hallway, sees me and stops.

"Hey," he says.

"Hey. Thanks for the salt and pepper shakers."

"You liked them?"

"They're cute. I didn't have any."

August rocks on his heels, looking at the tops of his boots.

"I was just finishing up some shots I took in Ottawa," he says. "Want to see them?"

"Sure."

In the darkroom it's quiet and contained. We look at August's photos of Ottawa's Parliament Buildings shot at night, their lights haloed in the fog.

"So how did the show go?" I ask.

August blows out a breath and turns around to lean against the counter facing me.

"It was great. No, more than great. I sold them all."

I look at him, surprised.

"I met so many people. Oh, and…" He touches my arm. "I got an offer for a show in Kingston next month. And an agent gave me her card. Said to call her. She wants to represent me."

"Wow," I say, swallowing on the word.

August rubs his face. "Everything's happening so fast."

"Well," I say. "I'd better get back to making my turkey salad for tonight." I open the door and stop. "Oh, your spare key." I pull the key out of my pocket and hand it to August.

He takes it and puts it in his pocket, then leaves his hand there. His expression is turned inward. "Maybe you should keep it," he says. "Just in case." He pulls his hand out of his pocket and gives me back the key.

The heat from August's hand has transferred to the metal when I close my fingers around it.

"Well, see you tonight," I say, picking up my grocery bags.

"Let me help you," August says, taking the bags from me.

We stop in front of my door and August puts the bags down. I fish my keys out of my pocket. Across the hall, I can hear Christian and Julie. A balloon pops, followed by an explosion of laughter. I rub my thumb along the smooth side of my door key.

When I turn to look at August, he is looking at me as if he's about to say something.

"I'm really happy for you," I say. "Everything that happened in Ottawa." I look down at the key in my hand. "Not that it surprises me. You're an amazing photographer."

August takes a step towards me and I look up.

His eyes are so earnest and blue. My lips are trembling.

August burrows his fingers in my hair, and presses his lips hard against my forehead and holds them there.

"I really missed you," he whispers hoarsely.

I try to speak, but my throat closes up, so I nod.

August steps back and releases a breath. Our smiles are shaky when we look at each other.

I touch his arm and leave my hand there. His hand rests on my waist.

"I'm glad you're back," I say. "Your studio looked really lonely when I was over there the other day."

August smiles, his hand tightening on my waist. "I wish you could have been there at the gallery. You would have loved it."

I nod. And then we just stand there looking at each other, unspoken words moving between us like an alternating current. August is breathing quick little breaths, his cheeks flushed. My heart is beating fast.

I don't know how long she's been standing there. She just appears at the top of the stairs, ghostly and still, the light from the stairwell framing her with a black outline.

I drop my hand from August's arm.

"What's wrong?" August pulls on my waist. He sees me looking down the hall and turns his head.

Caroline hasn't moved.

I see him close his eyes for a second, his lips pressing together.

I turn and unlock my door, pick up the grocery bags and go inside. When I close the door, August is still standing with his head turned, looking down the hallway.

A half minute later, I hear their footsteps on the stairs, then the front door of the building banging shut.

I drop the groceries on the table and look out the window. Dark mushroom clouds are puffing and growing in the sky above the pine trees. A dervish of wind is gathering deeper in the forest, building and building. The air is static and still, ready to crack and let forth a storm.

A jagged line of lightning splits the sky, flaring outside the window for a second, holding me in its spotlight, like a camera flash.

A few hours later, I hear music starting across the hall in Christian's studio. Outside the clouds are swollen, ready to split, but the deluge has yet to come.

When I walk into Christian's a while later, the party is in full, loud motion. The stereo is blasting U2 and people fill every corner, their paper plates heaped with food. Christian and Julie have hung cardboard turkeys with fat tissue paper butts from the ceiling. There are orange and red Christmas lights around the windows, blinking on and off like traffic signals. The fridge is entirely covered in green balloons, and there's a whole pumpkin sitting in the middle of Christian's green frieze´ couch. The room pulses with heat. I've entered Thanksgiving hell.

Christian sees me, and strides across the room.

"More turkey!" he yells, grabbing the bowl of salad out of my hands.

I stare at his head. He's wearing one of the fat-butted turkeys as a hat.

"Nice hat," I say.

Christian pulls the elastic under his chin and the turkey slides sideways.

"Julie made it for me," he says.

"Isn't she sweet."

Christian wiggles his eyebrows. "Isn't she?" He puts the salad bowl under one arm and takes my elbow.

Christian has set up his two worktables against the windows. One table is piled high with several whole roast turkeys, turkey sandwiches, turkey lasagna, turkey soup and a turkey casserole. The other table is filled with bottles of wine, soda, Scotch, towers of plastic cups, and in the middle, a large steel washbasin filled with beer bobbing in melting ice. A feast of excess.

"Eat!" Christian yells above the music.

"Drink," I yell back, pointing to a bottle of Scotch.

Christian slaps my back and rushes off to the kitchen to divert a disaster on the stove.

I see Mia coming towards me, and the tight ball of anxiety in my chest loosens.

"How'd your salad turn out?" Mia says, reaching for a beer.

"Too soon to tell. Nobody's keeled over yet."

Mia's outfit is entirely gray. She looks like a pearl.

"Well I can't *wait* to see what Queen Caroline brings," Mia says.

My face tightens.

Mia gives me a look. Then another one.

"What's wrong?"

"Nothing."

"Something's wrong," Mia says. "I can tell. You look... *wrong.*"

I tell her about the scene in the hallway with me, August and Caroline.

"But you weren't *doing* anything," Mia says, wringing her beer bottle with both hands.

Julie walks over to the table and saves me having to say anything more.

"I'm dying of thirst," Julie says. "Just ate some homemade turkey jerky." She clutches her throat and reaches for the soda water. Mia beats her to it and pours her a glass.

Julie is wearing a black and purple tunic printed with her signature pattern of fleurs-de-lis and diamonds.

"Christian's headgear is very becoming," I tell her.

She ducks her head and smiles. "Thank you."

Mia raises her beer bottle. "Good thing it's not hunting season."

Julie puts her arm around Mia. Mia barely comes up to her shoulder. "I'll tell him to beware of men in red plaid hats."

Julie keeps glancing over at the front door, presumably watching Christian in the kitchen.

"Oh, oh, gourmet alert," she whispers loudly.

Caroline walks into the kitchen carrying a large platter covered in tin foil. The large hump in the foil must mean another turkey.

The front door is open behind Caroline as she stands talking to Christian. I keep waiting for August to appear. Seconds go by, but the doorway remains empty.

Julie swishes the ice in her glass. "Where's August?"

Out of the corner of my eye, I see Mia turn and look at me.

I turn around and pour myself another glass of Scotch, forgoing the ice this time.

An hour later, August still hasn't appeared.

Mia, Julie and I have been standing around the food table, picking at one of the turkeys. The sky is popping with lightning outside the windows, but the rain hasn't come. I'm feeling a little drunk and the room has taken on a surreal glow.

We've been examining Caroline's dish. I was wrong. It wasn't a turkey. It's a huge salmon mousse *shaped* like a turkey. No one has the nerve to dig into it.

"It's so pretty, I don't want to wreck it," Mia says.

Julie examines it from different angles. "It's like a work of art. Like a sculpture."

There's a burst of laughter from the kitchen. Mia looks across the room and suddenly goes still.

"Holy shit," she whispers.

Julie and I turn around.

Christian, Brin and his friend Marley are circled around August. Christian is taking a case of beer out of his arms. Their heads are all close together, questions going back and forth. August has his head down, his hair falling forward. He looks up and the light hits his face.

The welt under his eye is still developing, red around the edges, starting to puff out below his eyebrow. A red line runs from the outer corner of his eye.

"Jeez-Louise," Julie says. "That's quite the shiner."

Food rises in my throat and I put my cup down on the table.

Christian is joking with August, all male bravado, bumping shoulders with him.

August is explaining something, using hand gestures.

"Ha, you moron," Christian yells, laughing as he slaps August on the back.

I look around the room and locate Caroline over by the stereo. She's holding a CD in her hand and talking to a man in a brown suede jacket.

"Whoa," Mia says, grabbing my arm. "Don't get into it with her."

"What's going on?" Julie says.

I'm already walking over to August, my legs unsteady.

Christian and August are bent over inside the fridge putting beer in the vegetable crispers. August straightens up when he sees me.

"What happened?" I say.

August looks to the side, wiping sweat off his beer bottle on the tail of his shirt.

Christian closes the fridge and laughs. "You won't believe it."

"Probably not," I say.

Christian frowns for a second, then laughs again. "He was trying to pry the lid off a tub of peanut butter. Doesn't know his own strength. His fingers slipped and he whacked himself in the eye." Christian puts his arm across August's shoulder. "Use a screwdriver next time, buddy."

August isn't smiling. His head is down, his swollen left eye hidden behind his hair.

Christian is waiting for me to laugh. When I don't, he rolls his eyes. "Come on. It's funny."

"Yeah, I'd buy it if August was left-handed."

Christian gives me a slit-eyed look. "Jesus, Anne, lighten up."

August looks at me for a split second and I see the embarrassment in his eyes.

"What the hell are you saying?" Christian says, moving in front of August protectively.

"Nothing. Forget it," I say.

I turn around and Julie and Mia are standing a few feet away, shocked expressions on their faces. Behind them, I see Caroline approaching, one hand on her hip. She pushes between Julie and Mia, brushes by me, and moves over to August, taking his arm.

August stares into space for a moment, then shifts away from Caroline, pulling his arm free.

Caroline looks at him, shocked, but it only lasts a second. She turns to me, her eyes blazing.

"I've had about enough of you. Why don't you leave him alone?"

August steps forward. "Caroline, don't."

The room is buzzing around me, pulsing and hot. I feel the storm rising inside, pushing its way upward and outward.

Caroline turns around and takes August's hand. "Come on, August, we're leaving." When he doesn't move, she yanks his arm.

"Don't do that," I say, moving towards her.

Caroline swings around and pushes me in the shoulder. "Get out of my way," she says.

"Whoa, whoa, everybody calm down," Christian says.

Someone turns the stereo off and the room falls silent.

Caroline faces me, her hands on her hips. Her eyes are blue, like skim milk, secrets swirling inside them, debating, deciding. Her mouth twists into a crooked smile and she leans towards me.

"I know all about you, *Anne*. You're a pervert. Taking pictures of fags fucking."

The blood drains from my face.

I look at August. His face is still. He knows.

"That's right," Caroline says. "You are a fraud."

"What the hell are you talking about?" Christian says.

"Stop it, Caroline," August says.

Caroline whips around to August. "Don't you dare defend her. Come on." She grabs his hand again. "We're leaving now."

"Anne, what's going on?" Mia says.

I can't think. Everything is crumbling around me.

"August, come on." Caroline pulls on his hand.

August's face tightens. He flicks his arm, shaking Caroline off. Her hand flies in the air. Everything goes still for a second.

Caroline's mouth is open in disbelief. She closes it, collects herself and looks at August. "I'm giving you one more chance. Or you can go back to the reservation and live with all the other losers."

August's face goes still and color rises in his cheeks.

Julie sucks in a surprised breath.

"Hey, now," Christian says, raising his hands.

My vision goes completely red and I feel myself leaving my body. My fingers curl into a fist, my arm tenses. Those words need to go back inside her. My arm recoils. I release it and my fist flies at Caroline's face, my knuckles landing solidly on her mouth. Her teeth are rigid as bones digging into my skin. Heat and pain shoot up my arm. Caroline's head whips back, my punch following through into empty air.

I drop my arm, every nerve in my body vibrating.

Caroline makes a gargling sound, her hands flying up to her mouth.

"Jesus Christ," Christian bellows, reaching out to catch Caroline as she stumbles backwards.

My hand hangs limply at my side, my knuckles burning, the blood pounding in my temples, my chest rising and falling.

I turn around and Julie and Mia are staring at me like I've just grown horns and a tail.

Caroline is making little "oh, oh" sounds.

"Take her," Christian says, handing Caroline over to August.

August hesitates, his arms at his sides. Caroline puts her head against his chest and he takes her by the shoulders, turning her around, away from him. As he leads her out of the kitchen, he brushes past me and I feel his hand touch the small of my back, an unseen gesture, a moth wing briefly brushing against a window.

Before my eyes can focus on anything, Christian has me by the arm. "You're out of here," he says, leading me over to the door.

"Christian no," Julie says.

"I'm sorry," I whisper.

"Get her some ice for her hand," Mia says.

"I'm sorry," I say again, only I can't seem to talk above a whisper.

Christian opens the door and pushes me through it. "Go cool off," he says.

The door closes behind me and I'm standing in the hall alone.

The feeling settles around me. Stripped of everything.

I raise my hands and look at them, foreign weights on the ends of my arms, instruments of violence, my own hands of doom.

CHAPTER NINE

Under The Silver Moon After The Storm

The pain in my hand throbbed in time with my footsteps. I could feel the skin on the back tightening as it started to swell.

A flash of lightning lit up the path ahead and made halos on the treetops. Ghost clouds sped across the sky, yellowed at the edges. The storm was moving eastward without leaving a single drop of rain.

The forest rushed and sighed around me as I walked deeper into the trees, following the path along the river to the park. I wasn't afraid. I felt a lot of things, but fear wasn't one of them.

Every step took me farther from The Factory, and as the cold air hit my face, I gulped it in. Waves of adrenalin kept coming. I'd hit her. Felt her lip split against her teeth. But then her words replayed in my head, *or you can go back and live on the reservation with all the other losers,* and I wanted to hit her again.

Another flash of lightning lit up the park as I walked out of the forest, a color photo for a second, then a black and white. The river was a shiny black strip in the dark.

What a fucking mess. My lie had been exposed. By now, I imagined everyone at the party knew who I really was. I felt sick thinking about their collective shock, that queasy gray moment when they realized they'd been deceived. Another wave of nausea made my jaw go slack. I wished I could erase that moment when I looked at August and saw that he already knew.

Walking across the park, a feeling of aimlessness came over me. I needed solace. And some purpose.

I had forty dollars in my pocket. The liquor store on Brock Street was still open. I bought the same brand of Scotch I'd been drinking at Christian's. The first swallow burned all the way down. The second spread down my arms. By the third, I had walked several blocks and was feeling calmer. Without realizing it, I had walked in a huge circle and was now heading up Hunter Street, back towards The Factory.

In the distance, I could see blue lights flashing on the front of the buildings on Water Street. When I turned the corner, I came to an abrupt stop, and almost dropped the mickey of Scotch.

In front of The Factory, a police cruiser was parked at the curb, the radio squawking, the light on top flashing a pale blue strobe. A group of college boys with excited faces stood across the street, their eyes glued to the front door of The Factory which stood open, yellow light streaming out on the sidewalk.

Fear shot through me like a narcotic rush.

Suddenly, an approaching vehicle, coming fast down Hunter Street, pinned me in its headlights. I froze. The vehicle sped through the intersection, then slammed on the brakes.

It was August's van. The passenger door flew open and Mia jumped out and ran towards me.

"Come on," she said, grabbing my arm and pulling me around the front of the van.

Through the windshield, I could see August sitting behind the wheel, his expression blank.

Mia pushed me in the passenger side door, closed it, then opened the side door and jumped in. August sped away, slamming me back in the seat, the bottle of Scotch banging against my chest.

"Not a good idea to go back there right now," someone said from the back of the van.

I turned in my seat. Julie sat on the floor in the back of the van beside Mia.

"Christian tried to stop her," Julie said, "But she grabbed the cordless phone and locked herself in the bathroom."

"Oh, Jesus," I said, grabbing the side of the seat as August swerved around a corner.

"We figured we'd better come look for you," Mia said. She touched my arm. "Is your hand okay?"

I shook my head.

"Well," Julie said, blowing out a breath. "And no offence, August, but she had it coming. I'd have hit her too."

We turned again and drove fast down Charlotte Street, the storefronts rushing past, the streetlights appearing and disappearing overhead.

"This is crazy. I should go back," I said.

August looked over at me.

"She wants you arrested," Mia said, rising up on her knees behind me.

"I shouldn't have hit her."

"She asked for it," Julie said.

"But now Christian has to deal with the police."

August jerked the wheel and the van bounced into the driveway of a gas station. He pulled up to the side of the building and jammed the gear in park.

No one said anything for a moment.

August looked in the rear view mirror, and then turned to me. "Just let her cool down for a while."

"I'm gonna call Christian," Julie said. "Get an update on the situation."

She opened the door and jumped out, walking quickly to the pay phone by the air pumps in front of us.

We waited in silence, while Julie used the phone.

She hung up and turned around, the wind blowing her hair across her face. Head down, she ran back to the van and jumped inside.

"Well?" Mia said.

"Christian's got a handle on it," Julie said. "Caroline told her version of the events. Then Christian gave his. Said everyone was dancing, it was crowded and Anne accidentally elbowed Caroline. Tempers flared. Yadda, yadda. Brin and Marley corroborated."

"Yeah, that's what happened," Mia said, bobbing her head up and down.

I looked at August. He turned his head away and looked out the window.

After a moment, he put the van in reverse and backed out onto the street. We drove at a slower speed through the quiet streets of Watson.

It seemed we were going to avoid the one thing no one had mentioned so far. But then Julie spoke as we neared Mia's house.

"So what was that crap Caroline said about fags fucking?"

"Yeah, Anne, what the hell was that all about?" Mia said.

My face tingled.

"Caroline is mad at me," August said. "She didn't want me to do the show in Ottawa."

I looked out the windshield, holding my breath.

"I don't get it?" Mia said.

August sighed and rubbed his face with one hand. "She blames Anne for me wanting to do the show. She's not a big fan of photography."

"Oh," Mia said.

"But what was that bit about fags fucking?" Julie said.

I opened my mouth to speak, but August jumped in.

"She thinks all photographers are perverts. Shooting nudes. You know like Mapplethorpe."

"Anne's never shot me nude," Mia said.

I released a breath and it came out as a nervous laugh.

Julie laughed and touched my arm. "And it's a good thing. We don't need to be seeing Mia in the buff."

Out of the corner of my eye, I saw August smile.

It was just after eleven when we dropped Mia at her house. She leaned over and kissed my cheek.

"You gonna be okay?" she said.

I nodded.

A few minutes later we stopped at the corner of Water and Hunter. The police cruiser was still there, the blue light swirling around the deserted street. A man in an overcoat, his pale green pajama bottoms peeking out from underneath, walked out the front door of The Factory and stopped, fishing around inside his coat pocket.

"Oh crap," Julie said. "Mr. Zion. Hope Christian didn't catch shit from him."

"He wouldn't evict us," August said. "He'd lose too much money."

I couldn't take my eyes off the swirling blue light on the police cruiser. I was having a Toronto flashback, the day I was arrested at the gallery, the day they snapped the cuffs on my wrists and led me away. In the back of the cruiser, I was shaking so hard, I couldn't sit up in the seat.

I felt like I might be sick. "You guys go on back. I'll get out here. I need some air."

August leaned over and grabbed my arm as I was reaching for the door handle.

"Wait," he said.

Julie cleared her throat and coughed. "I'm getting out," she said. "You guys drive around for a while. Call Christian's before you come back and I'll let you know if the cops are gone."

She opened the door and paused. "Don't worry, Anne. Everything's going to be alright." Then she slid out of the van and slammed the door.

We sat idling at the corner, watching Julie walk across the street and go in the front door of The Factory.

As soon as she was out of sight, the silence in the van became awkward. August and I were alone together.

We pulled away from the curb and drove through the intersection.

"Thanks for saying all that stuff back there," I said. "For covering for me."

August pulled into the alley that ran behind The Factory. "You want to go to the river?"

The van bumped over potholes into the back parking lot. Instead of parking, August turned towards the trees and nosed the van through the pines onto a rough path.

"We can't drive down here," I said, holding onto the seat as we bounced over a big rut.

"This is an old access road. It goes right through to the water."

Tree branches scraped across the roof of the van and the headlights moved up and down tree trunks as we tunneled deeper into the forest.

We got to a clearing at the end of the road, circled by pines, a blackened fire pit of rocks in the middle. I'd never been here before, didn't even know it existed. August stopped the van and the engine cracked with heat for a few seconds. Then he turned off the headlights and the forest went black. Quiet and black.

My eyes were adjusting to the dark. I saw a raccoon waddle across the clearing, stop to sniff the fire pit, then continue on into the trees.

August rolled down his window and the cool air that blew in was a relief.

He sighed once, turned in his seat to face me, and studied the seat belt stump beside my seat.

"This is my fault," he said. "I got you in the middle." He looked up at me. "Sorry."

It took me a second to respond. It wasn't what I thought he'd say. "It's not your fault." I looked away. "So how long have you known?"

He didn't answer.

"When did she tell you?" I said.

"You want to talk about that? Okay." He rubbed his face, shifted in the seat, resting his arm on the steering wheel. "Christ." He released a loud breath and dropped his hands into his lap. "I've always sort of known. The first time I met you I knew you weren't who you said you were. But when I was in Ottawa I found an article in *Mclean's* magazine. There was a photo of you and your mother walking down the street after your arraignment."

I couldn't take my eyes off his face. "I really wish you hadn't told Caroline."

August looked at me. "I didn't." He exhaled a breath and turned around in his seat and stared out the windshield. "She went through my knapsack and found the magazine. I brought it back from Ottawa with me. I told her I wanted it 'cause there was an article about Norval Morriseau in it. Later, when I wasn't around, she was looking through the magazine and found the article. Only, she thought I hadn't seen it. After she saw me with you this afternoon, she, ah… brought the thing about you to my attention. I guess she figured it was good ammunition." August paused and rubbed his face. "When I told her I already knew… she went crazy."

I closed my eyes. "And that's when she…"

August turned to me quickly. "Nothing she could have said would have changed my opinion of you. It was your secret to keep. For whatever reasons." He tilted his head. "Is that why you hit her?"

"No. I hit her 'cause of what she said to you, and what she did to your eye."

August sat up straight.

"August, I…"

He opened the door and jumped out of the van. I watched his dark figure walk quickly towards the fire pit.

I opened my door and climbed out.

"August."

I walked up beside him.

He kept looking straight ahead. "This is really embarrassing. I've been with her for five years. When I met her, she was so sure about the future, what her direction was, I believed it too. I thought I was supposed to be with her." He kept licking his lips and running his hands through his hair. "But, when I'm with you, my mind is quiet."

He released a quick breath and shook his head. "I read the future all wrong. There's a reason I was meant to find out who you were."

"And what was that?" I said.

August kicked a pinecone at his feet. "To let you go."

"What?"

August sighed and jammed his hands in his pockets. "You can't stay here, you know that. This isn't your home. Toronto is. You need to go back to your life. You had a career. You can't stay here pretending to be something you're not."

I shook my head. "I don't want to go back. I can't go back. Who I was, what I did... it's all gone."

August moved closer. "Then you start again. You start over as Albertine Hannah."

"I can't. I'm not ready."

August bent over and picked up the pinecone. He straightened up and threw it across the clearing, his arm whipping the air. "Remember when I said your place looked temporary? That it didn't look like you were staying? Now I know why. You were just taking a break till you figured things out." He took my hand, the swollen one. "You need to go home."

My mouth fell open. "Why the hell did you kiss me then?"

August touched my face. "I shouldn't have. You're not supposed to be here."

"No." I moved into his arms, feeling the warmth under his jacket. He held me so tight I couldn't breathe.

"Tell me what you want me to do?" he said.

I tilted my mouth up to his and took his bottom lip between my lips.

He hesitated for a moment, then his eyes closed and he kissed me hard, urgently, his hands pressing against my back.

The wind blew cold through my hair, August's mouth hot against my lips, the kiss building, the ground spinning beneath my feet. And it went on and on, and our hands were moving over each other.

Suddenly he drew in a breath. His hands came up to my face, cupping it. "What are we doing?"

I shook my head.

"Albertine," he whispered, drawing in quick breaths.

Hearing him say my name cut me wide open. I touched my tongue to his lips, wanting more of the way he tasted. His hands went into my hair, and his fingers pressed against my scalp. Then his mouth was on my neck, his breath hard in my ear. "I need to let you go," he said.

"Don't," I whispered, my mouth pressed against his cheek. I moved my head and looked in his eyes.

He went still.

I kissed his chin, the curve under his bottom lip. "Just keep saying my name. Make it real."

"Albertine," he said against my mouth. He drew his head back and searched my face for a long moment. "Okay," he said. Then he started kissing me for real, the kind of kissing that had a purpose.

I slipped my hands inside his jacket, working my way up under his shirt until I felt his warm skin and he drew in a breath that made me shiver.

A few minutes later, we were beyond stopping.

"Let's get in the van," August said, taking my hands.

"No," I said. "Let's stay out here."

The moon was tilting back in the sky, revealing stars and more stars, a sparkling doom looking down on us, touching everything with silver. I didn't want to contain the wildness in and around us.

August got the quilts we used for barbecues on the beach from the back of the van. He spread them on the ground in front of the fire pit. And when we lay down together, he pulled one of them over top of us and we turned in each other's arms.

I pulled off August's jacket, then his shirt, and then my own sweater and our skin met for the first time. We were drifting away, no longer connected to the earth, spinning towards the sky.

I thought he'd be shy. I thought the way he kissed was just a fluke. When I lay naked underneath him, I couldn't believe the skill and certainty of his hands. Like he was reading my mind and knew exactly how and where to touch me. His naked body moved over me, humming with energy, and I touched the soft skin on the back of his thighs, the curve in the small of his back, memorizing the details of his beautiful body.

He stopped and looked down at me, his eyes shiny with desire.

"Are you sure this is what you want?" His hand stroked my stomach.

I nodded and pulled him to me.

"Albertine," he said against my lips. His back arched under my hands. "Love," he whispered into my neck.

The sky had changed again to gray cotton, close and damp. August lay on his side, watching me in the dark.

"Albertine," he said.

I waited for him to go on, but he just closed his eyes slowly and cupped my face in his hands. He fell asleep like that.

I watched his face for a long time, the rim of shadow his lashes made on his cheeks, the divot above his lip. His essence was still inside me, a warm yellow ball spinning in my stomach.

I awoke a few hours later. The sky was turning a grayish blue, the color of an old negative. August's legs were still tangled with mine. I moved and he opened his eyes for a second.

"Hey," he said and pulled me closer, into the circle of his arms.

I finally drifted off to sleep, my world reduced to the warm burrow of our bodies. We had stopped time. My past had been dug up, an inert pile of bones, and the future was holding back, waiting for my okay to reveal itself. I was patient. The present was too beautiful to leave just yet.

CHAPTER TEN

Home

A mockingbird woke me, trilling like a cardinal. The sun was shining through the branches overhead and when I moved my face out of August's hands, he folded them under his chin without waking.

I sat up and felt the cold air slip in under the blanket and wrap around my back. It was cold enough to see my breath.

The van had circles of dew on the hood and in the shadows under the trees, a layer of mist floated close to the ground. The clearing was a flat color in the light of day, stripped of the mystery it held in the dark the night before.

I felt August's arm slip around my waist.

"You okay?" he said.

I slid back under the blanket and curled up against him.

"Yeah," I said, against his chest. His skin was soft and warm.

He nudged my head up with his chin and looked closely at my face.

"You sure?"

"What were you expecting?" I said.

His hands searched under the blanket, moving over my breasts, stopping just below my belly button.

I wanted him again in an instant.

He ducked his head under the blanket, sliding down my body and I swallowed, anticipating what he might do. He laid his head under my breasts and pressed his ear to my body, his hands holding my back gently, his fingers spread.

Then he turned his head and kissed my belly, softly, pressing his nose into my flesh.

His voice was muffled under the blanket. His lips vibrated against my skin, but I couldn't understand what he said.

He sat up and began feeling around for the pile of clothes at our feet.

"We should get out of here. It's freezing," he said, pulling his jeans on under the blanket. "I'll go warm up the van." He pulled his shirt on.

"Okay." I didn't move.

He touched my nose with the back of his hand. "Come on. Get dressed."

I watched him walk to the van and get in. When the engine roared to life, the sound broke the stillness of the forest and the mist seemed to scatter.

A half hour later we stood in my kitchen, the noon sun blasting in the window, making square patterns on the floor.

August poured a cup of coffee and handed it to me.

I put it down on the table and continued to study my hand. The swelling made my skin shiny and tight. My knuckles were tender, and there were three dents of broken skin from Caroline's teeth. I wondered if I should get a tetanus shot.

I sensed August's stillness and looked up. "What?"

He shrugged. "You haven't said much."

It was true. We hadn't spoken in the van on the short drive back to The Factory. I couldn't get a grip on the morning. My world had changed overnight and everything had that awkward out of place feeling.

"A lot to sort out," I said.

I flexed my hand and felt the broken skin open up. Truth was, I didn't like the way I felt about myself for hitting Caroline. The loss of control was embarrassing.

"Are you worried about last night?" August said.

"Which part?"

"I don't know. You tell me."

"I wish I hadn't hit her. I don't know how you feel about everything you know about me, and I'm not sure if Christian is mad at me. Generally my life feels kinda fucked up this morning."

August leaned against the counter. "My Uncle Leonard used to say that regret was a way of trying to change the past. You can't wish for what's behind you, only for what's ahead of you."

"Sounds like an optimistic man."

August nodded. "He was. You can lose yourself in regret. And Christian isn't mad at you. I'm sure."

He turned and poured himself more coffee. He stood with his back to me and drank.

I cleared my throat. "I guess what I really want to know is how you feel about the fact that I've been lying to you for a whole year about who I was and where I came from."

He didn't turn around. I watched the way his shoulder blades moved under his shirt, like little wings.

"Like I said, it was your secret to keep."

"That's not an answer."

August turned around. "I guess I don't understand why you *wanted* to be someone else."

"Because," I said "My name had become synonymous with child pornography. I loved my life in Toronto before everything happened. I loved my work. Then I was in the news everyday and suddenly people were nervous about hiring me. I lost my freedom."

August looked at the floor and nodded. "Do you miss it?"

I thought about my recent visions of Toronto in the fall, the swirling leaves and blue-lit streets. "Some things," I said.

August nodded again. "What are you going to do?"

"About what?"

"The future."

I looked at the square patterns of sunlight on the floor for a moment, then shook my head and shrugged.

August pushed himself away from the counter. "I'd really like to know. 'Cause…"

The phone rang cutting him off.

We both looked at it, and kept watching as it rang a second time.

I walked over to the filing cabinet and picked it up on the third ring.

"Hello."

It was Irene from Exit magazine.

"Hey. Guess what? That gorgeous photo you sent me? It's going full page in the Vancouver edition."

I looked at August. "You're kidding? What's it going with?"

"It's a story about the Tsawwassen First Nations and that land development they're doing on the B. C. delta. Building without a permit and now the city won't service them with water lines. It's a big mess. Aboriginals against Whites."

"Wow," I said, still looking at August. He was watching me. I smiled and his face relaxed.

"Albertine, you still there?" Irene said.

"Yeah."

"So where did you find the beefcake? Oh, my, God, he is gorgeous."

"Um… Someone I know."

"Okay, be mysterious. Anyway it's running in two weeks. You want me to send you issues? Or… listen, sounds like you're busy. Call me later and give me an address. Okay, gotta run. Toodle-loo."

She hung up and I held the phone for a moment before putting it down.

"That was the magazine I used to work for in Toronto. I sent them that photo I took of you. They're going to use it."

"That's great," August said. He ran his hands through his hair and looked around the room.

I shook my head and couldn't stop smiling. "Yeah, it's been a while since I had anything out there. And hey, it's going with a story about the Tsawwassen First Nations."

"Really," August said, and his mouth twitched, which might or might not have been a smile. He rubbed his arms and walked to the table. "Well, I've got to go do some stuff. I promised Christian I'd return the empties from the party."

I watched him put his coat on.

"August?" I said. "I'm not sorry about last night."

He tucked his mouth in and nodded. "Good," he said.

I followed him to the door.

He stood close to me, and pulled a dried leaf from my hair. "I'll see you later."

I wanted to kiss him, but he turned, opened the door and walked out.

I stood for a minute listening to his footsteps going down the hall. His door opened, then closed again and I was alone.

For a year my art had existed in obscurity. It had been a long absence. The thought of one of my photographs being in a magazine again was thrilling. I felt validated. Not only that, it was validation as Albertine Hannah.

I looked out the window at the trees, their black trunks receding into the depths of the forest. That's what I'd been; someone lost in the forest for a year.

You can lose yourself in regret. I guess that's what I'd done. Lost myself to the extent that I'd created a new identity. I regretted leaving Toronto, leaving my mother, regretted not staying and fighting for my reputation and while I didn't regret photographing Eric and Daniel, I did regret putting the photograph in my last show. It was the wrong time and place for it, and I believe it wouldn't have shocked and offended if it had been shown in a different setting. I regretted lying about who I was when I moved to Watson, though I didn't regret coming here. I regretted that I hadn't treated my friendship with Mia, Julie and Christian with honesty. If I had it all to do over, I would have been braver.

I did not regret last night with August. I thought about the way he touched me and knew he could make me burn forever.

Maybe I did regret it. When August said my name, I felt whole again for the first time since I'd left Toronto. But I couldn't be whole in Watson.

Here it was, the price I had to pay. I thought I'd been so clever, inventing a temporary life, like I was renting something I could return. Well I couldn't return all of it. I couldn't return August.

I drove to the emergency room at the hospital. My hand was turning an ugly shade of red and was hot to touch.

The doctor who looked at it asked how it had happened.

"I accidentally knocked someone in the teeth," I said.

"Hmm…" he said, turning my hand over and pressing my palm. "That's interesting. A fellow brought a young woman in here last night with a busted lip. She said someone had belted her in the mouth."

"Really," I said.

The doctor raised his eyebrows. "Really. Some coincidence, eh?"

He gave me a tetanus shot and sent me home.

I knocked on Christian's door just before dinner, but he wasn't home. There were no sounds from next door either. I wondered where August was and felt the ache start inside me. Everything was in pieces. I needed to sort them out and see if they could be put back together into something resembling a life.

I sat in front of the window and watched the sun set on the pine trees, the light fading around me until it grew too dark to see, and even then, I didn't get up to turn the light on.

Hours later, I went into my bedroom, feeling my way in the dark, stripped off my clothes and crawled into bed. I closed my eyes and fell into a deep sleep immediately.

Sometime later, a sound woke me up. I struggled to open my eyes. A weight pressed down on the bed and I sat up gasping.

August sat on the edge of the bed. He turned and took my shoulders in both hands, and brushed the hair out of my eyes.

I leaned against him and put my face in the hollow of his neck, breathing him in. He had an earthy forest smell I couldn't get enough of.

The lump in my throat swelled and I held onto him tightly.

August kissed my forehead and my chin and my mouth. Then he kissed me again, differently, and in an instant we were burning in each other's arms.

He undressed quickly and slid under the blankets and I felt the full length of his warm body press against me.

His hair brushed against my shoulder as he lay on top of me, and he touched my forehead with his fingers and said, "Stay."

He did not speak again until he said my name in a fiery whisper, "Albertine", his body rigid for a moment, then collapsing against me, while his arms held me so close, I forgot for a moment we were once separate people.

Near morning another sound woke me and I sat up in bed. The sky was the color of gunmetal and the room was bathed in a pearly light. I listened for a moment, trying to remember the sound and my dreams came back to me, something about water, the hissing spray of a waterfall.

I looked down at August. He lay on his stomach, his head turned away from me, the blanket around his waist, his back and shoulders uncovered.

I noticed a mark on the back of his shoulder and leaned over for a closer look. I'd never noticed it before. He had a small tattoo, the size of a silver dollar. It was the earth, tiny green continents surrounded by blue, but a jagged line ran down the middle and it was separated into two halves. I touched it with my finger.

August rolled over and opened his eyes.

I reached around and touched the tattoo.

"Tell me about this?" I said.

August took my hand, raising it to his lips and kissing my swollen knuckles. "I got it when I was fifteen," he said. "Wasn't a great time in my life."

"What does it mean? It looks like a divided world."

August ducked his head and examined the tips of my fingers. "That was me. A foot in both worlds. Didn't belong on the Rez 'cause my father was white and didn't belong in town 'cause I was from Curve Lake."

"So where do you belong now?"

August closed his eyes and pulled me closer, releasing a sigh. "Right here. I belong right here."

I rolled over in his arms and pressed my back up against his chest. His breathing deepened and he was asleep again.

I lay awake for another hour, watching the gunmetal sky start to glow and the pearly light stretch across the floor to the bed.

It was possible that your sense of 'home' wasn't something you could control. It wasn't always a place. It was whom you spent your time with.

I closed my eyes and didn't wake up until someone banged on the door at eight a.m.

I was out of the bed and across the floor before I was fully awake. The banging continued, rattling the glass.

"Anne? It's Christian. You need to open your door now."

I stopped, realizing I was naked. "Just a second," I said.

I ran back to the bed and grabbed my jeans from the pile of clothes on the floor. August was already pulling his pants on.

Christian banged on the door again. "You need to get out here."

"Coming," I yelled. August threw me his t-shirt and I pulled it over my head, while he jammed his arms into the sleeves of his shirt.

"Fire," August said, jumping up from the bed.

"Shit," I said, looking at my heap of camera equipment in the corner.

August got to the door first and threw it open. I held back, expecting plumes of smoke to come rushing in.

Christian stood in the hallway, his arms folded across his chest. When he saw August, his face registered surprise for a second, then he unfolded his arms and pointed at the door.

"Seems we have a vandal," he said.

I could already see the black letters spray-painted across the bottom of the door.

August stood back and looked.

The paint had run in a few places, but the word was clear and in huge letters.

PORNOGRAPHER

A tremor went down my spine.

Christian was staring at me. "Any thoughts?"

I opened my mouth, then put my hand over it.

August walked back to the bed, sat down and reached for his boots. "She's gone too far."

Christian cleared his throat loudly. "What the hell is this all about?"

"I'll go talk to her," August said, getting up from the bed.

Christian stepped in the door. "Wait a minute there, buddy. Caroline did this?"

August patted Christian's shoulder. "I'll paint the door this afternoon."

He walked up behind me, took my shoulders, kissed the top of my head and strode out the door.

"August." I ran out the door after him. I stopped him at his door. "Don't."

"I need my jacket," he said, turning the doorknob.

"She might hurt you."

August closed his eyes for a second, then released a sarcastic laugh. "Wouldn't be the first time."

Christian came down the hall. "Hey, guys. This is starting to creep me out. Has she gone psycho?"

August opened his door and grabbed his jacket off the wall hook.

"I'll be back," he said. He walked down the hall, putting his coat on.

I watched until his head disappeared down the stairs.

"Anne?"

I turned around.

Christian was rubbing his forehead nervously. "Look, I have to go to work now. But, should we be worried?"

I shook my head and forced a smile on my face. "Can we talk about it later?"

"Okay," Christian said, backing down the hallway. "I'll be home at five. Maybe lock the front door."

I paced for an hour, and every time I pictured the spray-painted word on my door, a sick feeling rose in my throat. I'd thought I was past all that.

During my trial in Toronto, someone put a bumper sticker on my car that said, Support Pornography – Hug A Child. I spent hours trying to peel it off and ended up painting over it. But every time I looked at the raised rectangle of black paint, I saw the words burning underneath.

A circle of heat bloomed in my chest. How dare she do this? It was so childish.

I put on my coat and walked towards Caroline's house on Brock Street. I had no idea what I'd say to her.

Halfway there, I saw August coming down the sidewalk towards me.

I ran to close the distance between us.

"She wasn't home," he said, when I reached him. "And I checked her office. They said she was taking a few days off. She might be at her parents, but if I went out there they'd shoot me before I got to the front door."

"Oh," I said. August was chewing his lip, his eyes cast to the side. My anger seemed too simple all of a sudden.

A part of me was relieved August hadn't confronted Caroline, but there was an irritating string hanging, scratching at my neck. I wanted closure, for myself and August.

"I've got a job this afternoon," August said. "Got to take some insurance claim photos."

I studied his face and noticed a tightness under his eye where the skin was turning a spotted rainbow of yellow and purple. My chest constricted. How foolish I'd been thinking he could walk away from her so simply. It was going to be more complicated than that, maybe an inch-by-inch withdrawal. I hated the thought that I might be making it harder for him.

"Well, I'm going to go to the hardware store," I said.

August looked at me.

"Paint," I said.

The area under his eye tightened a little more.

I touched his hand and his knuckles were cold and chapped. "I'll see you later?"

He nodded, his smile forced.

I turned to go.

"Hey," August said, reaching for my arm. "I'm really sorry about all this."

"It's not your fault," I said.

When I got to the hardware store it bothered me that August felt responsible. Caroline had painted my door, but it was going to take more than a coat of paint to cover the marks she'd left on him.

When I got home, I looked at the door and felt weary of my past. My year in Watson seemed like just another extension of my long wait for it all to be over. Becoming someone new hadn't been a rebirth. It had been a gestation, my ugly secret a trembling egg waiting to hatch. I put the quart of paint on the kitchen table and made a pot of coffee.

A while later I heard Christian and Julie's voices in the hall.

"Oh my God," I heard Julie say outside my door.

"Yeah. Nice, eh?" Christian said.

I heard the door being unlocked and them going inside.

Twenty minutes later, I walked across the hall and knocked on Christian's door.

"Hey," Julie said. She pulled me in the door. "Chris, Anne's here."

Christian's studio smelled like turkey. The remnants of the party were everywhere, dirty paper plates and empty cups on every surface.

Christian walked out of his bedroom, pulling a clean t-shirt over his head.

"Hey," he said. "We really need to take care of that door."

"Yeah, I know."

Julie shook her head. "Boy, August wasn't kidding when he said she thought all photographers were perverts."

Christian walked over to the fridge and opened it. The green balloons on the door hung flaccidly. "You want a beer?"

"Sure," I said.

Christian handed me a beer bottle and stood back, picking the label on his bottle.

"I need to ask you something?" he said.

"Yeah?"

He breathed out. "August didn't hit himself opening a tub of peanut butter did he?"

I didn't answer. Julie was dabbing at a spot on her tunic.

Christian looked up at me. "Did she hit him?"

I hesitated a moment, then nodded.

Christian sighed, "But it was an accident right?"

"No," I said.

Christian looked at me, then glanced at Julie. His face blanched. "You knew about this?" he said to Julie.

"Yes," she said. "And it wasn't the first time, either."

Christian shook his head, the muscle in his jaw clenching. "No way. He wouldn't put up with that."

"But he has," Julie said.

Christian drained his beer bottle. "I don't believe it," he said, spinning around and opening the fridge.

Julie turned to me and raised her hands.

Christian closed the fridge door. "Okay, so what's really going on? Why did she paint your door? I'm not buying that she's just pissed about you decking her, or is jealous 'cause something's going on between you and August."

Julie sucked in her cheek and squinted at me. "She knows something about you, doesn't she?"

"Yes," I said.

Christian tilted his beer bottle at me, urging me to talk.

I took a deep breath and plunged in. "I'm not from Vancouver. I'm from Toronto. And I moved to Watson 'cause about a year and a half ago I was arrested for child pornography."

"Holy shit," Christian said.

While I sat on the couch and Christian and Julie stood in the kitchen, I told them everything.

When I finished, Christian was staring at me with his mouth open. Julie stood very still.

I sat with my knees pressed together and my fingers tightly laced.

Then Christian blinked and turned his head to the side. "You..." He breathed through his nose. "I can't believe you didn't trust me enough to tell me the truth. You think I'm not open-minded enough to see that you got a raw deal?"

"Chris, calm down," Julie said. She smiled at me. "I think it's kind of intriguing. Inventing a new identity, starting over somewhere new, being mysterious."

I closed my eyes and pressed my hands to my forehead. "It really hasn't been much fun."

"Honestly?" Julie said. "I thought maybe you were hiding from your boyfriend and that's why you were so private."

"There wasn't really a boyfriend," I said.

"Jesus Christ," Christian said. "So that's why you always paid your rent in cash and never got any mail. I thought you'd had a horrible childhood or something and didn't want to talk about it. Man, I thought we were better friends than that."

Julie turned to him with her mouth open. "Christian, please shut up. She's the same person she was an hour ago. Just a different name."

I got up from the couch. "I don't know what to say to make it better. I can't change what I've done. But, I'm very sorry."

Christian walked over to the couch and flopped down on it. "Man, I'm just… it hurts that you thought I'd judge you. You should know by now I'm not like that."

I walked to the door. "It's one of my many regrets," I said.

Christian sat up, and pressed his lips together. "Hey, do me a favor. Don't tell August. This would kill him. He doesn't like being lied to."

I opened the door. "He already knows."

The paintbrush shook in my hand as I painted over the letters. I sat on the floor inside my studio, the door propped against the wall.

Across the hall, Christian had his stereo on loud, some kind of frenzied jazz.

In my mind I saw bridges burning everywhere. And in my mind, I was leaping ahead of the collapsing structure, trying to outrun the fire. I saw Watson falling over the edge, the flat land folding and disappearing.

At nine o'clock that evening, Julie phoned me from The Underdog. Music blared in the background and Christian was working his anger out on the dance floor.

"It's been a day of rude awakenings for him," Julie said, yelling into the phone. "He comes across as liberated, but it's hard for him to accept that August let Caroline hit him. It just makes him uncomfortable that a man could be the victim of abuse."

"Well, he cares about August," I said.

"He does. But so do you." There was a pause on the line and the band ended a song, the applause crackling in the receiver.

"Hey, Julie? Don't tell Mia. I want to tell her myself."

"Sure. Take care."

She hung up and I missed the sound of the music coming through the phone.

I stayed up late, waiting for August to come home.

At two a.m. I woke up feeling the bed move. August lay down on top of the covers fully clothed. He stared at the ceiling.

When I moved, he flinched and turned to look at me.

I rolled over and raised myself on one elbow. "I'm sorry I lied to you."

August lifted his arm and bridged his fingers on his forehead. His chest rose and fell rapidly. I laid my hand on his chest and felt his heartbeats pounding in tense little bursts.

"Let's just sleep," he said.

I removed my hand from his chest. "I wish I hadn't lied to you," I said.

August said nothing. After a moment, I rolled over, away from him and closed my eyes, pretending to be asleep.

Near dawn, August got under the covers and pressed his naked body against my back. We made love, slowly and quietly, the rising sun stripping the room of darkness, bit by bit, and just as August came, his face was revealed in the pale glow reaching through the window, touching his eyes and mouth with warm gold.

"Don't let go," he whispered, holding me tightly.

When I woke hours later, he was gone.

Around noon, I heard his van pulling into the back parking lot. When I looked out the window, he saw me and waved, then ran to the fire stairs, climbing them two at a time.

I opened the door and he glanced briefly at my paint job before entering in a rush of cold air and the smell of leaves.

"Hey," he said, kissing my forehead. His cheeks were flushed with cold.

I handed him a mug of coffee.

August sat down at the table and slipped his jacket off. "I drove out to the Rez this morning."

"Really? How come?" I sat down across from him.

He looked across the room to the window. "I don't know, I woke up this morning and really wanted to see this spot on the lake I used to go to when I was a kid. It has the most amazing stand of birch trees. Looks like an ice castle." He shook his head and drank from his mug. "I don't know. It felt good to be there. The Rez has changed for me."

"In what way?"

He ran his hands through his hair and looked at me. "Today I didn't feel like an outsider."

"You no longer have a foot in two worlds, eh?"

August scratched his shoulder. "I don't know."

I pictured us under the trees in the forest, wrapped around each other and wondered which world it had seemed like to August.

He stirred out of his thoughts and sat up. "I'm going to go over to Caroline's again today and talk to her."

"You don't have to."

"Would you rather I didn't?"

I looked in my coffee cup. "I don't know. It seems pointless. But then again, maybe you have some stuff to work out with her."

"Yeah, I do," August said, his eyes distant as he looked out the window.

After August left, the phone rang.

It was my mother. She asked the question I knew she'd ask. Did I think I might be coming home for Christmas this year?

I didn't go home last year and it caused quite a stir in my family.

I told her I thought there was a good chance I'd be there.

After I hung up, I pictured Christmases with my family, especially when my father was still alive. There was something comforting about personal history and a sense of continuity in familiar traditions. No matter how much life changed, there was a corner of the heart that remained untouched. Your sense of *home* was something you couldn't control.

It was late afternoon when I saw August's van pull into the back parking lot. I watched him get out. He didn't look up and wave this time.

He'd just closed the driver's side door, when a blue Honda Accord skidded into the parking lot, turned sharply and lurched to a stop beside the van. The door swung open and Caroline jumped out. August walked toward the back staircase, as if he'd been expecting her.

Her voice was high and muffled as she called out to him, the wind blowing her hair across her face. She was wearing a pale blue wool coat and it flapped open as she ran after him.

She caught his arm at the bottom of the stairs, hugging it to her whole body, her forehead pressed against his shoulder. August looked up at the sky for a moment. He said something and Caroline raised her head, her face looking up into his, hopeful and pleading. Her hand slid down his arm and clasped his hand tightly. Then she smiled, urging him forward and together they climbed the stairs.

A moment later, I heard the back fire door open and their voices fill the hallway.

"Don't worry, I'm not going to tell anybody," Caroline said. "Yet," she added.

"I think that would be best," August said.

"You're still mad," she said.

"I'm not mad," August said.

Their footsteps stopped just outside.

"Oh. She painted the door," Caroline said. "Good."

August sighed loudly.

"Are you going to tell her?" Caroline said.

"Tell her what?" August said.

Caroline's voice got low. "About us?"

"Come on," August said, their footsteps moving down the hall.

A moment later, August's door creaked open and their voices faded as the door shut behind them.

I stood there, blood pounding in my temples, watching a tidal wave of doom rush towards me.

I ran all the way down to the diner, needing to talk to Mia. I kept seeing August and Caroline standing at the bottom of the stairs, pressed together. *It wasn't over. It wasn't over.* The words kept repeating in my head.

I thought about his body next to mine, the sweetness of his mouth, the way he'd said my name, giving himself completely. In the moment of surrender, it had felt like there was nothing between us but the heat of our skin. But there had been. Caroline existed inside August, like a tumor that couldn't be cut away cleanly. My desire for him had been my Sword of Damocles. His exquisite love had given me back my joy. And now the ax had fallen on my head.

As soon as I got to the diner, I saw Mia through the window and realized I hadn't told her the truth about who I was yet. I couldn't do it right now. My nerves felt like frayed wires.

I kept walking past the bus terminal, all the way down to Stewart Street where there was a Tim Horton's. The light was fading and the air was damp and cold. I went into Tim's, got a coffee and a maple iced donut, then sat and looked out the window until the sky changed from indigo to black. An hour later, I got up and walked back to The Factory.

It was warm inside the front door and I stood for a moment letting the heat from the radiator at the bottom of the stairs warm my hands.

A door closed upstairs and staccato footsteps came towards the top of the stairs.

Her head appeared and when she saw me, she held her hand up.

"Hi," Caroline said, coming down the stairs, her shoes rapping against the wood.

She got to the bottom and I saw her mouth for the first time up close. Her lip was swollen, though she'd covered the broken area with makeup.

"Sorry about your mouth," I said.

Caroline nodded and touched my arm. "I know you are. Listen, let's just call it even. Everything's been worked out." She nodded towards the stairs. "August's fine with it. And I know all about your little rendezvous with him. It's fine. We all went a little crazy for a few days. I don't blame him."

"What?"

Caroline tilted her head back and forth. "You know," she said, a sheepish grin on her face. "Truth is he needed to get it out of his system. Good. Now we can get on with things."

"Get on with what?"

Caroline smiled and patted the front of her coat. "I just found out. I'm pregnant."

My stomach collapsed like I'd been hit with a wrecking ball.

I swallowed the dryness in my throat, watching Caroline's face, her glowing expression, as if all was right with the world.

"Excuse me." I brushed past her to the stairs and started up them, each step harder and higher to climb.

As I neared the top, Caroline's voice echoed up the stairwell.
"Bye, Anne, er... I'm sorry, Al-ber-teen."

Was she lying? Did it matter? No.

I looked around my studio. I had a nagging feeling that there was something I needed to do, but the harder I tried to focus, the more it slipped away. My ears were ringing and I couldn't stop the sensory memories of August's hands on my back, his mouth on my neck.

Someone knocked on the door and the spinning stopped.

I opened the door and took a step back.

"I need to tell you something," August said. He stood in the doorway, his eyes flicking off my face as soon as he looked at me.

"No you don't. I already know."

His face sagged. "You do?"

"I ran into Caroline when I was coming in."

August closed his eyes. "Oh, shit." The words came out in a soft rush of air.

"This was a huge mistake."

August looked at me quickly. "You mean that?"

"Yeah."

His face twitched, then froze in a puzzled expression. "I'm sorry you feel that way."

"I've got to go," I said.

"Go where?"

I shook my head.

"Albertine?"

I looked at him. "Please don't call me that. I'm not Albertine here. I never have been."

I closed the door and as soon as I heard his footsteps going back down the hall, I knew I was leaving.

It was surprising how little clothing I had once I'd packed it all in my duffel bag. I looked at the sagging sides and wondered where everything had gone. I'd thought my life had gotten fuller here.

I moved around my studio methodically. I had to get out of there. I looked at the kitchen table and the sight of the two coffee cups August and I had drunk from this morning were like props from a play two characters had acted out.

It had all been an illusion. A sweet, temporary illusion.

When I walked past August's studio, he opened the door.

"Wait a second," he said. Then he saw the bags in my hand and his eyes widened. "You're really going?"

"Yes."

"This is crazy." He ran his hands through his hair. "What the hell were we doing this morning and the night before and the night before that? You're telling me you regret all of it? Wished it never happened?"

"Yes," I said.

I took one last look at his China blue eyes. They were still pure and innocent, but held the portent of a complicated future.

"You said I needed to go home," I said. "You were right. It's time."

August moved towards me. "It's not over."

"You're right. You and her? It's not over."

"That's not what I meant."

The front door of The Factory opened and voices came up the stairwell.

August started to say something, but was interrupted by Christian and Julie running up the stairs, laughing about something.

"Whoa," Christian said, when he got to the landing and saw my bags on the floor. "What's going on?"

"I'm going," I said. "I'll send you my rent for next month."

"What?" Julie said, looking at August.

"How long are you going for?" Christian said.

"Don't know," I said, picking up my bags.

"Anne, wait a second," Christian said. "I apologize for being such an ass yesterday."

"You're not an ass," I said. I touched Julie's arm. "Take care."

I took one last look at August. He stood in the doorway, rubbing a spot on his forehead hard.

"For Christ's sake, August," Christian said. "Say something. Don't let her leave."

"I can't," August said, looking at me, his face empty. "I have to let her go."

"Bye," I said, not looking at any of them.

Then I walked down the stairs leaving a stunned silence in my wake.

I stood outside The Factory for a moment. A light snow had started to fall and there was a vacuum of silence surrounding the black-stemmed trees that escaped into the low purple sky. There was sadness in the quiet and regret started to form a knot in my stomach.

It was cold and dark when the bus left the streets of Watson and pulled onto highway 401 headed for Toronto. The long windshield wipers slapped the swirling snow off the front windows in a steady rhythm. Inside the bus it was dark and warm, the passengers held motionless by the hypnotic hum of the wheels.

I sat in the plush purple and green seat, weighed down by weariness. It was over.

As soon as the bus pulled out of the terminal, I felt my bond to Watson break. I was no longer rooted there on the quiet streets. I felt a years worth of my life snap and retract into nothing.

CHAPTER ELEVEN

The Trial

When I was younger, I believed that photography made you immortal. I remember looking through my grandmother's photo album at my grandparents, aunts, uncles and cousins, all of them held in a sepia-toned permanence. And earlier still, were previous generations immortalized in silvery tin daguerreotypes, their frozen expressions a brief moment of arrested time before they released their poses and resumed living and breathing.

I liked to imagine the moment before and after the photograph was taken, the sound of their voices, their movements in their stiff white dresses and heavy wool suits. For me, they lived on in an alchemy of bromine and mercury. Without the photographs, there was no evidence.

Eighteen months ago, I went to court for my arraignment. I felt detached, the whole event so surreal, it was like it was happening to someone else.

My mother came with me, dressed in her 'serious suit', the navy wool blazer and slacks she wore when she had to go see her lawyer or accountant. We'd argued that morning about what I was going to wear. She wanted me to buy a suit, one like hers, something "respectable".

I'd heard her on the phone the night before with my brother, Arvo. She wanted him to come to court, saying something about "strength in numbers". Arvo made an excuse about having a prior appointment. My mother said, "if you won't go for your sister, couldn't you at least go for me?" A few minutes later I heard her slam the phone down.

She insisted on taking a cab to the courthouse on Queen Street.

"I hate driving downtown," she said. "And we'll never find parking."

In the cab she fussed with her purse and the scarf around her neck. "When did your brother get so selfish?" she said out of the blue.

I could tell she didn't expect an answer. Then she said, "I'm glad your father isn't here" and in my detached state, I thought she'd said, *I wish your father was here.*

"I wish he was too," I said.

She raised her eyebrows, paused in thought, then shook her head. "Albertine, if the lightning bolt hadn't killed him, this would have."

For the rest of the cab ride we said nothing.

I was sure the arraignment was just a technicality, cut and dried. I clearly wasn't a pornographer. I figured the judge would take one look at the photograph, roll his eyes at having his precious time wasted, and send me home, free and clear.

I was wrong.

The child pornography laws had recently been redefined, the jail term for conviction increased up to ten years. My lawyer was to plead my case on the grounds of artistic merit. The crown prosecutor was to plead on the grounds that depictions of sexual acts involving someone under the age of eighteen, or who *appeared* to be under the age of eighteen, would incite pedophiles to commit acts of molestation and feel justified in their behavior. Art or not, my photograph appeared to show a child being fucked by an adult.

The crown prosecutor was very convincing. I saw the judge's eyes change when the prosecutor uttered the words; *the protection of the innocent is paramount.* That sealed it. Art or not, the safety of children came first.

When my lawyer raised the issue of freedom of expression, things looked hopeful. The judge agreed. He withdrew the charges against the gallery owner and me. My mother smiled and squeezed my hand. But it wasn't over. *The protection of the innocent* was still ringing in the judge's ears. If I couldn't be put on trial, then he would put my photograph on trial. It took a few minutes for the courtroom to settle down after that announcement.

"Can he do that?" my mother kept asking my lawyer.

He could. And he did.

There were two whole months in between my arraignment and the trial. Two months is a long time to wait for judgment. My whole life was put on hold. I stopped working completely. Every time I picked up my camera it looked like an instrument of doom. My eye no longer framed potential beauty. I was in a holding pattern, waiting to have my identity reinstated.

And then the publicity started to grow. My upcoming trial wasn't first page news, but it became a running story for weeks in the middle section, right near the editorials. They ran the same damn picture beside every story, me and my lawyer walking out of the courthouse the day of my arraignment. It was April, a raw, sun-split day, the wind whipping my hair across my face, like I had something to hide. They cut my mother out of the picture.

During the first three weeks of the trial, there was an endless parade of the crown's witnesses, the child psychologists who talked about pedophiles and their love of *pictures*.

The protection of the innocent is paramount. The crown's lawyer repeated that over and over until the lines blurred in my mind and I wasn't an artist anymore. I was someone who wasn't protecting the innocent.

As the court recessed every day, I watched the bailiff remove my photograph from the easel at the front of the courtroom and carry it away to the basement vaults where they kept the evidence.

169

I imagined it lying next to bloody knives, sawed-off shotguns and other horrific instruments of crime. Each trip down, my photograph was subjected to corruption, like throwing an accountant into a jail cell with murderers. And each trip back up to the courtroom, the photograph looked more depraved; as if it were succumbing to the influence of the company it was keeping.

I thought of Eric and Daniel's beautiful faces staring in the dark, their sleeping innocence so defenseless and vulnerable, they would be prey for someone.

Her name was Margaret Perifoy.

Why did she do it? She was in a position of authority. I saw her everyday, slightly pudgy in her blue bailiff's uniform, lifting my photograph off the stand, holding it in front of her so that she was forced to look at Eric and Daniel all the way down to the vaults. I stared at her tight blond perm and mannish hands for two weeks in a perfunctory way, never seeing beyond the uniform, never guessing at the turmoil that twisted inside. Her bland face never gave away the anger and despair she felt about her son.

When she burned the photograph, and the negatives I'd been forced to surrender, it wasn't child pornography she was trying to destroy. It was homosexuality.

I'd expected there would be some people who'd object to Eric and Daniel being gay. But when the focus became child pornography, there was no mention that the photograph showed two naked men together.

Margaret Perifoy found out her son was gay six months before the trial. She was devastated when he told her his lover's name was Danny. For six months Margaret Perifoy prayed and went to confession, but nothing could erase the stain of mothering a homosexual. For two weeks she had to look at my photograph, daily reminders of what her son must look like in the arms of his lover. During the third week she snapped.

She took the photograph down to the vaults and decided to end her torture. She smashed the glass and the frame, ripped the photo out and lit the edges with her Bic lighter. She watched as the image of unnatural love blackened and curled, their faces burning like souls of damnation purified by flame and oxygen, turned to dust and blown from this world. She was holding the already melted negatives when the smoke alarm went off, alerting two policemen who were having coffee upstairs. They came running down the stairs, but it was too late. Margaret Perifoy crumbled when they touched her, falling to her knees, sobbing incoherently, her hands clasped together, reaching towards the ceiling, beseeching God to accept her act of sacrifice in exchange for the salvation of her son's soul.

My lawyer screamed for a dismissal on the grounds that there was no longer any evidence. The crown lawyer argued halfheartedly. His job had been done for him. Vigilante justice. The judge rapped his gavel hard, his face etched with anger, and granted a mistrial. He commented dryly, that instead of trying me for child pornography, he'd probably have to try Margaret Perifoy for arson.

My lawyer wanted me to sue the court for defamation of character. I didn't have the will to do anything but grieve.

My mother held a celebration party, but it was a hollow victory. The groups who had supported me – The Toronto Arts Council, Artists Against Censorship – reacted as though my fuse had fizzled before I was shot out of the cannon.

The trial was over, but I had neither lost, nor won. I was free, but not cleared. I was still an artist, still a pornographer. My identity hadn't been reinstated. It had been expanded.

If I was still an artist, then where was my art? I would never be able to recapture that moment when Daniel moved closer and took Eric in his arms. A moment of my life had been removed, sliced out, leaving a still, quiet hole.

My photograph was gone. Eric and Daniel no longer lived on in an alchemy of bromine and mercury.

I tried to go back to work, but the damage to my reputation became evident immediately. I was hired by a conservative magazine to photograph the mayor. I was un-hired when they decided to include the mayor's children in the photograph and someone brought my recent child pornography trial to the mayor's attention. There were a few other incidents, some nasty phone calls to my mother's house, where I was staying. Then someone set fire to my car. The police said it was random violence. I wasn't sure.

Two weeks later, I left Toronto and went to my Aunt Clara's in Kingston. Away from Toronto, the battle began in my head. Each day, from the moment I woke up, till I went to sleep, I had a running conversation in my head with Margaret Perifoy. Each day I'd explore a different angle, a new defense as to why she shouldn't have destroyed my photograph. I revised my dialogue until it was perfect, an unbroken diatribe full of wit and confident anger. Margaret Perifoy would remain mute while I assaulted her with clever perfect words. It gave me brief periods of resolve. But the argument stayed in my head and therefore had no end. The next day it began again, this time more perfect, more powerful, seeking an end, seeking the closure that would never come because I would never get what I wanted. I would never get my photograph back.

When I left Kingston to stay with a friend in Bobcaygeon, I felt like I'd never be able to take another photograph like In The Arms of Daniel. I'd never find that moment again where my subjects were perfectly out of pose, where spontaneity tripped the heart and exposed the soul.

Then I met August and he gave me that moment.

After leaving Watson, I spent the first three weeks in Toronto at my mother's in an energized routine. I made her breakfast every morning, walked down to Danforth Avenue and bought the paper and browsed at Book City, then I spent the rest of the day reading like I was starved for words. I did a few assignments for Irene at Exit, making enough money that I wasn't totally sponging off my mother.

November came and went. Only in my dreams did Watson

resurface. My ties to everyone there felt severed, everyone except August. He was the one thread left hanging. In my dreams he reached for me and like a delayed bruise, it only hurt afterwards when I remembered what had happened.

My sister Angela came over frequently to check up on my mother and me, and there were weekly dinners with my brother Arvo and his wife, Jill. My mother loved having me back home. And as Christmas approached, she mentioned more than once how complete it would be if Aaron came home for the holidays. Family. Everything seemed normal.

I was in transition when it came to my photography. I was craving a different direction. I started going to the library and studying books by other photographers. My creative well felt a little dry, but I could feel inspiration trying to break the surface.

It was after a month back home that I realized I was in a holding pattern. I wasn't really moving on being back in Toronto. It was more like I was resting up for the next journey.

It took me until the first week of December to write Mia and tell her the truth about who I was. I kept putting it off throughout November, not wanting to unearth any memories of Watson. But guilt nagged at me. I owed her that much. I truly regretted leaving before I had a chance to talk to her.

The second week of December I got a letter back from Mia.

Dear Anne,

Sorry, it feels weird to call you Albertine. Thank you for your letter. Julie did tell me everything after you left, but it was good to hear it from you too. I wish I could have said goodbye to you. I'm not sure exactly why you left so quickly. Was it because of August and Caroline? Or were you homesick for Toronto?

I hope it wasn't because of August and Caroline.

Caroline kept up her charade about being pregnant so she could keep her claws in August. It didn't work. She was lying about it the whole time. She wasn't pregnant at all, though she claimed the pharmacy had made a mistake with her pregnancy test.

August has changed since they broke up for good. He got really drunk with Christian, then he got quiet and has stayed that way. He doesn't smile the way he used to. But he hasn't been home much lately. He got an agent and has done two gallery shows already. He's doing a longer tour after Christmas, which will include some galleries in New York State!

I'm really sorry about all the stuff you went through with your trial and while I wish you had told me the truth about it, I sort of understand why you didn't. I'm just glad you did move to Watson even if it was only for a little while.

Christian and Julie are officially dating. They're both happy and well. Christian still hasn't rented out your studio and I'm thinking about moving in there next month if you're sure you're not coming back. Are you?

Still working at the diner. I'm thinking about taking some art courses at Trent U. in the spring. I miss you. Please write back. I want to know what you're doing and that you're happy. Love Mia

After I read Mia's letter I pulled out the copy of *Exit* magazine that had my photograph of August in it. I'd looked at it briefly when it came out, but got an ache so intense seeing his face, I put it away immediately.

I opened the pages and there he was, unchanged, stuck back in time, that afternoon in my studio when he kissed me for the first time and then gave me back my lost creativity.

He was free now. Free of Caroline, free to wander the country showing everyone his beautiful photographs. He'd moved on.

Was I ever going to go back to Watson? I couldn't now.

I needed to move on too.

CHAPTER TWELVE

The Magic Body

The week before Christmas I put up the tree in my mother's living room, and when we'd finished decorating it, I was struck once again how a yearly event could have such continuity when there were all those days in between where our lives had grown and changed. I could string together every Christmas since I was five like they were a succession of days. But it was a trick of time. Christmas was a touchstone, an illusion we clung to out of fear that our lives had lost the way back from where we had begun.

The year was coming to an end, bringing closure. When I thought about the New Year, it seemed full of possibility, an endless plane of new snow without footprints.

The past year had been the slow denouement of my former life. Leaving Watson had been the final act. I was home now and home was immortal, the past living on through pictures and Christmas memories, but the future waited like a photograph I had yet to take.

The day after Christmas, I took out my portfolio and looked at my photographs from the past year. I hadn't looked at them since leaving Watson. It was like looking at someone else's work. Being back in Toronto, I had shed Anne Hanes, the person who had taken those pictures. I was Albertine again, but not the same Albertine as before.

Magazines used to hire me because my photographs had a unique style. I developed my shots with a signature border, a jagged blurry frame, instead of a hard edge of white paper. People loved that look. They asked for it again and again. I used to etch my name, ALBERTINE, into the still-wet print.

My style had changed in the last year. For obvious reasons, I'd given up signing my photographs.

Except for the photograph I'd taken of August, there was a lack of evidence in my work. I'd given up the personality of my photographs. And like I had lacked a conviction during my trial, my work lacked a conviction.

The week between Christmas and New Year's stretched out with constant sunsets. The sun seemed to begin its descent as soon as it came up. I'd wake up and then I was watching the light fade to orange across the living room wall. I slept so much that week, my mother thought I was sick and brought me toast and tea in bed.

Toronto was beginning to make me sick. The morning after going to a party with my friend, Irene, I woke up feeling horrible. I went back to bed for a few hours and when I woke up again, it was like a new day. I wasn't bursting with energy, but there was a tight coil inside, a teeth-gritted kind of determination.

I was suffering from camera withdrawal. My hands were twitching from lack of use. My eye kept framing shots and I'd hear the shutter clicking in my head.

The pictures my eye kept framing were of myself. Every morning I looked in the mirror and instead of doing my ritual, I measured my expressions. There was a progression each day. As the shock of leaving Watson subsided, my emotions seemed to solidify. There was a definition forming around my mouth, a deepening in my eyes, a sharpness in the angle of my jaw. My shoulders were framed in the mirror as if they'd been drawn, all clean lines of shadow and light. I looked at myself naked and saw the density of my flesh, as though my skin was tightening over my bones, filling in the recesses over my ribs and under my breasts. I watched the reflection of my hands, clenching and unclenching, the tendons moving like snakes under my skin.

I set up my camera in my Grandfather's old attic studio and tried some test shots. I positioned a stool in front of the camera, close enough that I could reach the cable release. Then I snapped a few head and shoulder shots, then a few of my hand.

When I was done, I felt excited. I couldn't wait to develop the film and see what would emerge on the paper.

The only problem was I didn't have a darkroom. I'd run into an old friend who had a studio in the same building where I used to have mine. Gary was a food photographer; *Toronto Life* and *Homemakers* magazines were his big clients. He had a really nice darkroom and offered it to me in the evenings.

I went over the next evening to Gary's place at Richmond and Bathurst. He'd left a key for me under the mat and when I opened the door, the studio smelled like rotting fruit. There was a platter of brown pineapple and rusty apples on a table covered with a bright green vinyl cloth. Gary had such a strange job, photographing gourmet food spreads that had been doctored with shellac and shaving cream to make them look more appetizing and perfect. He obsessed over the lighting for roast beef the way I used to obsess over lighting for fashion models.

When I developed the shots I'd done the previous afternoon, the results were interesting mistakes. The stool had been off-center and I ended up getting half of my face and one shoulder. But the proportions were interestingly symmetrical. In the head and shoulder shots, my single eye was the focal point. In a normal face shot, you have a complete person with a balanced personality. Half a face reveals one extreme of the emotional scale.

There was a game we used to play when I was a photography

student at Ryerson Polytech. We'd take shots of models from magazines and cover up one eye and then the other. We had a theory that
everyone had a kind, warm side and a cold, evil one. Eyes are not
identical twins. We all have a light side and a dark side.

The photograph of my half face showed my dark side.

The shots of my hand startled me. I got moved looking at my
hand curled over my knee. My eyes started to tear up and I was over-
come with a profound sadness. My emotion unnerved me. It was past
one a.m. I quickly cleaned up the studio and went home.

New Year's came and went, but I was so consumed with my new
project, I glided right over the marker and slid into January.

I developed a routine. Everyday, I got up, ate breakfast, then
went back to bed for a few hours till I could wake up again and feel
that burning determination. It wasn't there when I woke up the first
time and yet I couldn't seem to sleep past eight o'clock. Something
was brewing inside me. My dreams at night were becoming vivid
and big, complicated scenes and busy conversations going on around
me. For some reason the turmoil didn't scare me. I'd lived in fear so
long, it was a welcome change to sit back and calmly wait for whatever was going to hatch.

My mother wondered what I was doing upstairs in the attic
studio, but she let me work in peace. I stayed up there secretly shooting
my self-portraits until I could go to Gary's studio and develop them.

Sometimes I finished shooting early and went out to buy supplies
at Henry's Camera down on Church Street before heading over to
Gary's. After a week, my self-portraits were starting to get good, so I
indulged in some expensive fiber-based paper to make my prints
look grainy. I'd been shooting myself in black and white to force the
emotion in my face and body to the surface.

On Day Two I got some shots of the top of my head, cutting off
the border just below my eyes. I centered the stool this time to get
both eyes, light and dark, good and evil.

On Day Three and Four, I shot just my hands and feet. The feet were hard. I had to do a lot of experimenting and ended up standing on the stool to get a level perspective. I wasted a lot of shots trying to point the camera down on the tripod, but I kept getting my knees in the shot and I wanted my feet to appear separate from the rest of my body.

On Day Five, I switched to my limbs. I did some of my leg elevated away from my body. Then I did my outstretched arm. I liked the ones where I caught the web of my armpit. It was scary at first, stripping off my clothes and modeling nude for myself, but when I developed the shots later, the vulnerability in them made me feel liberated. The next day I did my stomach and breasts.

By the end of the week, I had my entire body, segmented and documented. The fiber-based paper was worth the expense. It gave the illusion of the emulsion being painted on the paper, the surface three dimensional, with the lighter areas jumping off the paper, while the darker areas were recessed into the crevices of the fiber.

I went back to my face again, shooting smaller areas, a cheek, half a mouth, an eyebrow raised, furrowed, relaxed. I was inside it now, unaware of time moving around the clock, days rolling into the next, getting up, eating, going back to sleep, getting up again, shooting, eating, developing.

Sometimes I ran into Gary at the studio cleaning up his food for the day, cakes and tarts, pizzas and hams. I actually hated the smell and after he left, I would open all the windows and air the place out.

My nights got longer and longer, stretching into dawn, until I was there when the sun came up. One night I stayed so long, Gary came in for work the next morning and shook his head at what he must have assumed was my obsessive devotion to my photography.

Was it devotion? It didn't feel like ambition. I wasn't shooting for anyone but myself. There was no objectivity. I couldn't ask my model to pose differently because I was the model. I was joined to my camera, inside the body, behind the lens and in front of it at the same time. I had become the camera, the film, had crawled right inside and laid myself on the negative.

After two weeks, I gave the shooting a break and concentrated on the prints. I liked the texture of the fiber paper, but I wanted something to stimulate the black and white images. I began experimenting with paint. Acrylics were too stiff and I ended up with cloudy prints that looked like someone had spilt milk on them. The paper absorbed the liquid if I tried to water the paint down. Watercolors were closer, but I couldn't get the right tone without adding too much color.

I went back to the library and once again poured over books on photography, studying the evolution of various techniques. Finally I found what I was looking for. The photographer's name was Jack Spencer and when I turned the page and saw one of his photographs I almost fell off my chair. The photo was just the torso and the tops of the legs of a young black boy. He was holding an enormous silver fish across his chest. The scales of the fish glowed and yet the boy's skin was a warm fuzzy brown tone that blended into the background.

I searched the shelves and found a whole book of Jack Spencer's photographs. It explained his technique of using oleopasto, an oil paint manipulator and then a combination of earth-toned paints that were brushed over the print, and then wiped off.

I was so excited, I took a cab to Queen Street to my favorite art supply store and bought a huge amount of paint and oleopasto and a half dozen brushes in various sizes. I had a wonderful feeling of nostalgia buying art supplies, remembering all the times I'd gone there for my Grandfather to buy canvases and oil paints for his portraits.

Later on, I went back to Henry's Camera and bought Gary a big supply of fixative and toner and paper, and as a twisted way of thanking him for letting me use his studio, I also bought him a fruit basket.

I worked in my Grandfather's old studio, experimenting with the oil paint manipulator. I got so consumed in it, the next thing I knew, it was almost February.

My mother liked me working at home all day.

"You're painting?" she said when she saw all the supplies I'd bought. "That's wonderful, dear."

I think she was relieved I seemed to have more purpose than when I'd first come home.

I had a complete set of photographs, enough for a show. But I didn't want to have a show, at least not in Toronto. Toronto was starting to feel used up. It wasn't home anymore. Home was just a memory, a head full of snapshots.

Filling my portfolio again had given me the chance to dig inside my own garden and see what was down there. I had a documentation of myself, every inch of flesh and bone. I wasn't Anne Hanes anymore, but I wasn't the old Albertine either. I was a new version of Albertine, the one committed by the camera and she was solid, real and permanent, many pieces of evidence in black and white film.

I had a future somewhere. It just wasn't going to be in Toronto.

Out of the blue, I had a memory of August.

I was having lunch with Irene down on Queen Street. I was poor company and wished I'd cancelled. Halfway through lunch, my food was suddenly unappealing. I'd been living on ginger ale for days because my stomach had been acting funny. Irene reminded me it was flu season and maybe I was catching it.

I left the restaurant and was walking down Queen Street when I noticed a couple standing in front of a Gap store. She was laughing, her head thrown back, while he smiled and held onto her arms. Then he took her face in his hands and she stopped laughing. They looked in each other's eyes, oblivious to the bustle of people walking around them on the sidewalk. He cupped her cheeks tenderly and kissed her.

I remembered August's hands cupping my face at the train station, his warm fingers pressed against my skin. My lips burned remembering his kiss and the way the sun fell on the top of my head, warming my hair.

Something heavy and painful expanded in my chest. Then it felt hollow, a cavern of loss nestled under my ribs.

I walked for blocks, holding back a flood of memories afraid I would drown. I tried to erase the couple, the way his hands looked on her face, picking out each detail from my memory like tiny shards of glass.

By the time I got home, I was exhausted and went to bed. My dreams were worse. It was like home movie night, endless reels of Watson memories, August building a fire on the beach, August smiling into his coffee cup at the diner, August lying next to me, his feet curled overtop of mine.

When the films ran out, I fell into a deep black well of sleep and didn't wake up until seven o'clock the next morning.

I awoke with one clear thought. I hadn't just left Watson. I'd lost August. He was running into the future, traveling far and wide.

I needed to start making some plans.

At my lunch with Irene, I'd mentioned that I needed some jobs. I was running out of money fast. Irene said that the Vancouver office of Exit was looking for a new photo editor and pushed me to call the chief editor and talk to him.

"You're not happy in Toronto," she said. "Why not give the west coast a try?"

I called the editor, Trey Fortune, the next day and in one phone call I not only had a job, but a future destination. I was moving to Vancouver.

"You're going to move all the way to the west coast?" my mother said when I told her. "When are you leaving? Are you sure you want to go that far away? I'll never see you. Will you still come home for Christmas?"

"Of course I will," I said, trying to appear certain.

The truth was, as soon as I decided to take the job, I started worrying I was making another reckless move. It was scary to think about living in a new city where I didn't know anyone. I didn't want to run away from Toronto. I wanted to leave with the calm confidence that I was pursuing my future.

By the first week of February I had found an apartment hotel in Vancouver, had sent the editor at *Exit* some photos, and had decided I was going to drive there. I would be leaving two days after Valentine's Day.

There were just a few things to take care of first.

I had been feeling funky for weeks now. It could have been the messy process of realigning myself and the excitement of doing my self-portraits. It was similar to the way I felt when I was first starting out as a photographer, working all night, totally buzzed being behind the camera. Or maybe it was just being back in Toronto, away from Watson, away from the burden of trying to be someone else. I decided I should go see a doctor.

I went to the doctor. I didn't like what he had to tell me.

The last time I'd left Toronto, my mother helped me pack. She was anxious to see me go and be delivered safely into the arms of her sister in Kingston. It was after the nasty phone calls, and after my car was torched.

It was different then. I was removing myself temporarily until things calmed down and I could resume my life in Toronto. Vancouver wasn't a temporary relocation. I was moving on as the new Albertine, the one I'd created with my camera, every part, limb and inch of flesh documented, like puzzle pieces that could be assembled into a whole person, my new skin stretching over my body, the casing over my new soul.

I put five hundred dollars down on a used van. I would drive through the flatness of the prairies, rise over the Rockies and descend to the ocean's edge in Vancouver. And when I arrived there, my new life would begin.

I spent a week getting ready, doing laundry, some camera equipment maintenance, buying a supply of oleopasto to take with me in case I couldn't get it in Vancouver. I studied maps and plotted my route. I needed to focus on the next step and avoid looking too far ahead. There were too many questions there. I thought about next Christmas and whether I'd come back to Toronto. Everything would be different by then. My life would be altered.

On Valentine's Day, two days before I was to leave, I went downtown and got my hair cut.

The back of my neck felt prickly and naked as I ran my hand up into the blunt ends of my hair. Nick the Barber had been in a generous mood. I said "an inch" and he took a mile.

I walked down Queen Street past Spadina Avenue, watching the lunch crowd through the windows of the cafes. There were hearts and white lace, red roses and happy couples everywhere. I didn't want to think about love.

I walked past my old apartment, across a side street from the Cameron House, the coolest club in the eighties and nineties. I'd lived there when I was going to Ryerson. It had been a great time to live on Queen Street. The Gap and Le Chateau hadn't forced the artists and booze cans out yet. I used to drink every night at the Cameron House and dance in the back room where the bands played, sweating in the dark, drunk on my youth.

A block down I passed the video store and stopped to look at the posters in the window. The sidewalks were crowded and people moved past me, their faces intent on getting to their destination.

I heard someone calling my name.

"Albertine!" It was closer to a shriek above the noise of traffic.

I turned and there was Irene, weaving through the crowd, her brown hair blowing off her shoulders. She wore jeans and high-heeled boots, a brown padded satin jacket, and a fuchsia and kiwi silk scarf. Even dressed casually, Irene always looked like a fashion plate.

She had a newspaper under one arm and a Styrofoam coffee cup in her other hand.

"I just saw your guy," she said, slightly out of breath. "Whew, like your hair cut." She flounced my hair.

"Thanks. What guy?"

"The guy in the picture."

"Doubt it. He's not in the picture anymore."

"What?" Irene squinted her eyes at me. "Yeah, it was him. I didn't put two and two together. *Exit* is reviewing his show tonight. I didn't know what he looked like till I saw the ad. Here." She handed me her coffee cup and unfolded the newspaper under her arm. She leafed through the pages, which kept folding in the wind. "Here it is... August Killdeer... *Wild and Untamed*. Jesus, who comes up with these names?" She handed me the newspaper. "See, it's him and the show is at the gallery below my apartment."

I took the newspaper from her. There was a quarter page ad with a photo of August and the dates, time and location of his show at Artspace.

The newspaper felt electric in my hands. I stared at the image of August, his face turned to the side, the wind blowing his hair behind his head. His eyes were focused on something in the distance. Before I could stop it, excitement bloomed in my stomach, a whole flock of twitchy butterflies touching their wings against my insides.

"So we're going, right?" Irene said.

"Yes," I said.

When Irene and I walked into the gallery a few hours later, I thought of all the reasons I shouldn't have come. There was one obvious one, but I told myself I could handle it. I was leaving for Vancouver in thirty-six hours. I had a safe commitment for the future.

"Jeez, what is this, a wake?" Irene said.

The gallery was empty. Under the blindingly bright lights the white walls were stark, except for the photographs, large black frames and blurs of black and white images.

There was a murmur of voices from the opposite side of the room. The art reviewer from Exit stood talking to a woman in a long black tunic. She had severe black hair, cut into a bob with Anne Rice bangs. They were hovering over a long table covered in stiff white linen, rows and rows of plastic cups filled with white and red wine, a platter of cheese cubes impaled with toothpicks, and as a sad ode to Valentine's Day, a bowl of red candy hearts. Whoever had set up the table had been expecting an army that was obviously late.

August was nowhere in sight.

"Oh, there's Terry," Irene said, walking across the room, her eyes scanning the photographs.

I focused on the wall in front of me, then moved closer, not sure I was seeing what I was seeing. I walked over to the first photograph on the left side of the gallery.

It was a portrait of Mia. Her face stared out of the frame, a background of hazy gray swirling around her head. It was steam from the diner grill rising behind her. She was in her waitress uniform, and it must have been at the start of her shift because her apron was pristine and white.

I moved to the next one, another large format print in black and white of an aboriginal woman dressed in beaded buckskins, one leg raised on a fallen birch tree, her face looking off into a stand of pine trees.

I moved quickly to the next and the next. Christian, bare-chested on the beach holding a log over his head, his breath a white cloud escaping from his mouth, his skin wrinkled with cold. Joe the bartender at the Red Dog, sitting on a case of beer in the alley behind the club.

I kept moving around the perimeter of the room, looking at one after another, all portraits of people from Watson. There was Julie, wrapped in yards of material, her bare shoulder poking out of the folds, Barb and Wendy sitting on the front steps of the Red Dog smoking cigarettes, Mr. Sepic in the diner, sitting at his table staring into his cup of coffee while the people around him were blurred in motion.

I stopped before the last wall, my pulse beating under my jaw. August had changed the fundamental style of his photography. He had shot *people*. Not only that, he'd made them come alive the same way he used to make his buildings and trees come alive. There was a deep intimacy in each photograph. He'd achieved what every portrait photographer wanted to do, expose the soul behind the face.

I looked under the photographs at the small white typed cards. They each had the date and time, which was August's habit, but I was surprised to see he'd also titled them.

Christian's portrait was titled **"Hercules on the Beach"**. Julie's was **"Wrapped Beauty"**, Mia's **"Angel of Sustenance"**. They'd all been photographed in November and December of last year.

"It's his newest series."

I turned around startled. "What?"

The woman with the Anne Rice hair stood behind me, smiling. "He just finished this new series. I'm Sylvia Truman, the gallery owner."

"Albertine Hannah," I said, shaking her hand.

"Oh," she said, tightening her hold on my hand. "Of course. It's an extreme pleasure to meet you. I was at your show. The one... you know, that got..."

I nodded and she released my hand.

"Wait, you're also the one..." She paused and pointed to the wall I hadn't looked at yet. "... In that gorgeous photo. It's one of my favorites." She squeezed my arm. "So why am I telling you about his latest series. You know August, obviously."

I walked over to the wall.

My face filled with heat. There I was, curled on my side, wrapped in a blanket, fast asleep with the early morning sun touching the forest around me. I felt the fear an alcoholic must experience when they see the evidence of something they don't remember.

It was that morning in the forest. August must have taken the picture before I woke up, then gotten back under the blankets. I didn't even know he'd had his camera with him.

I looked at the card underneath the photograph. **October 11th – 8:04 a.m. – "Aurora Borealis".**

Had there been Northern Lights that night? Or did August think I was like those lights, a brief shimmer in the sky that disappeared quickly?

"That one's special, hmm?" Sylvia had been standing beside me the whole time.

I nodded and forced myself to look away from the photograph. "Um, where is August?"

Sylvia arched her eyebrows. "Who knows? He left here this afternoon. Said he'd be back in a few hours. He seemed..." She paused and put her finger on her lip as if she wasn't sure she should say anymore.

"Seemed what?"

"A little nervous about tonight. I do hope there's a better turnout." She grimaced and looked around the room.

A bell dinged and a rush of cold air swept into the gallery as the front door opened.

I turned around and felt a smile spread across my face.

"Anne? I was hoping you'd be here."

It was Julie, followed by Christian. Christian looked at me and smiled sheepishly. They walked into the gallery, ducking their heads at the bright lights, their eyes scanning the walls, their faces lit with the timid kind of excitement you have when you're from a small town and are thrust into the glare of a big city.

Julie strode across the room and hugged me. "Wow, you look great," she said, holding me at arms length.

"Hey, stranger," Christian said. He hesitated and then bear-hugged me.

"How are you guys? That's great you came into town for this." I looked at Christian. I'd never seen him wear a suit.

Julie ducked her head and giggled. Christian cleared his throat.

"Well, actually," Julie said, "We got married at City Hall this afternoon."

"You what?" I looked at them both.

Christian nodded, his lips pressed in, but he couldn't hold back a smile.

"Wow. Congratulations," I said and hugged them both, again.

"So where's Nature Boy?" Christian said, looking around the room.

"Not here yet," I said.

Christian gave a mock sigh. "Figures he'd show up late to his own party."

"There's wine," I said.

We moved over to the table, and I handed Christian a glass of white, which he drank in big sips. I handed another one to Julie.

"So cheers, you guys," I said, raising a glass. "Here's to the newlyweds."

"To old friends," Julie said. "It's really great to see you, Anne."

Irene cleared her throat loudly behind me. "Aren't you going to introduce me...*Anne?*" She elbowed me in the back.

"Irene... Julie and Christian. Friends from Watson. They just got married."

"You brave souls," Irene said, toasting Julie and Christian. "And on Valentine's Day to boot."

Thirty minutes later, half a dozen people had shown up, mostly friends of Sylvia's, but the place had more of a party atmosphere.

I was listening to Irene tell Christian and Julie a story about her former roommate, a musician named "Rocky," when I glanced out the front window of the gallery and saw someone looking in. As soon as our eyes met, he turned away and walked to the front door.

I watched the door open and August walk in, brushing snow off the sleeve of his jacket. He glanced around the room. His eyes settled on Sylvia, laughing with her friends in the back corner.

I felt light-headed, the muscles around my mouth twitching. The past stirred in my belly, and heat climbed up my legs.

"Hey," Christian said, pointing, then waving to August. "You should shoot your barber."

I couldn't stop staring. It was August, but it wasn't. He'd cut all his hair off. His eyes were the same deep blue, but the angles of his face were more defined. He'd grown into his skin, lost his boyish softness.

"Oh my goodness," Julie said, quietly. "He cut off all his beautiful hair."

"So this is the infamous August," Irene said, nudging my shoulder.

August walked over to us, his eyes fixed on Christian.

Christian grabbed him and hugged him hard. "It's been ages, man."

"I'm so glad you guys are here," August said, his voice muffled against Christian's shoulder.

August released Christian and hugged Julie.

"We did it," Julie said.

August stepped back and smiled. "You got married? Wow."

August turned to Irene and raised his hand. "Hey."

Irene grabbed his hand and pumped it hard. "I've heard so much about you. Irene. Great to meet you."

When August turned and looked at me, his face changed. It was subtle, but I noticed it.

"Albertine," he said and nodded.

My voice was locked in my throat. I nodded and forced a smile. There was a tremor in my neck and I was afraid my head was jerking.

"I should go talk to Sylvia," August said, eyeing the wine on the table. "But I need one of those first." He walked over and grabbed a glass of red and took a big gulp. "You guys gonna stick around for a bit?" he said, looking at Christian and Julie.

They both nodded with giddy smiles.

We watched Sylvia embrace August excitedly and introduce him to all her friends. There was a lot of hand shaking and reverent smiles. August thanked them one by one, humble and beautiful.

Christian and Julie were beaming with pride.

Irene was uncharacteristically quiet.

I was realizing I'd made a big mistake in coming.

A while later, Julie and Christian went to look at their portraits, while Irene stood with me, picking at the cheese plate.

"Aren't we the pathetic duo?" she said. "Valentine's Day and neither of us has a date."

I looked over at August. He was still talking to Sylvia and her friends. Just as I'd predicted, the men were smiling at him admiringly, and the women were galvanized by his beauty. August didn't need a date on Valentine's Day. He was loved by everyone. Pain filled my chest. I should have just left Toronto with my memories of him.

"Well," Christian said, walking up with Julie. "We have a honeymoon to start."

Julie blushed. "We're staying at the Holiday Inn."

"Yeah, I'm gonna call it a night," Irene said. "It's a long way home. I live all the way upstairs." She turned and pulled me into a hug. "So you're off day after tomorrow? You'd better write."

"I will," I said.

"Where are you going?" Julie said.

I felt self-conscious. It seemed like I was always leaving them. "I'm moving to Vancouver. Got a job at *Exit* magazine."

"Aren't you the itchy-footed one?" Christian said.

Julie subtly elbowed him.

"Guess I'll go too," I said. "You guys want to share a cab?"

Julie looked at Christian. "Sure."

When Christian went to tell August we were all leaving, Julie leaned into me and said, "Does August know you're going to Vancouver?"

I shook my head.

"Oh," she said. "I won't mention it if you don't want me to."

I shrugged indifferently. The ache of regret was starting, gravity pulling me away with a breath-snatching yank.

"Okay," Christian said, walking up rubbing his hands. "August is going to share a cab too. He's staying at a studio Sylvia has near here. Some place called the Art Cube."

Irene nudged me. "Oh, Albertine used to have a studio there. Didn't you?"

"Yes," I said, just as August walked up to us.

His face was flushed. "Are we all leaving?" he said.

Outside the gallery, Irene said goodbye and went upstairs to her apartment.

The four of us stood on the sidewalk, no one saying anything for a long moment.

"So, I'll hail a cab," I said.

I stepped between the parked cars and looked down the street.

Behind me I sensed some silent communicating going on. Gravity was yanking me hard while I fought to stay upright and intact.

We were wedged into the cab, all four of us in the back seat. August was next to me, his thigh pressed against my leg, the warmth of his skin coming through his jeans. His hand rested on his knee, inches from mine, a band of heat pulsing between us.

I was coming apart inside, molecule by molecule crumbling. August used to be open to me. Now it was gone. I had to let go. My future waited. My future. It was hard to think about it without thinking about August.

The Art Cube was just around the corner, at Richmond and Bathurst, the same building where Gary's studio was and where I'd spent most of January. The cab got there in what seemed like seconds.

There was a brief argument over who would pay the fare. I settled it firmly.

"I'm the last stop. I'll get it. Think of it as a wedding gift."

I got out of the cab to let August out.

"Call us tomorrow," Julie said to August. "Maybe we can get together for brunch."

August leaned down into the cab and said goodbye.

I stood on the sidewalk, trying to think of something to say.

August turned to me, his face impassive. "Why did you come?"

I opened my mouth in surprise. "I… wanted to see your show. It was amazing by the way."

August nodded and looked down the street. "I wish you hadn't."

My eyes burned and the ground looked blurry. The cab idled at the curb, raising huge clouds of exhaust into the cold air.

"Wow that hurt."

August sighed and ran his hand through his hair. "Sorry. That was rude. I just didn't expect you to be there. Kind of caught me off guard."

"Kind of caught me off guard when I found out this afternoon you were having a show here."

"I would have sent an invitation if I'd known where you were."

I blinked and felt the wetness on my lashes start to freeze. "Did you *want* to know where I was?"

August blew out another breath impatiently. "I don't know. I don't know if I want to get used to seeing you again."

"Well, you don't need to worry about that."

The taxi honked its horn. Julie leaned out the door of the cab. "Anne, do you mind if we go? You guys keep talking."

"No, I'm coming," I said.

I turned to go. August grabbed my hand. His fingers burned against my skin. I looked at him, confused.

He blinked slowly, but said nothing.

"Okay, we're going," Christian yelled from inside the cab. "We'll call you tomorrow, August. Good luck in Van..., um, see you, Anne."

August's eyes were fixed on me. He looked over my shoulder for a second and nodded.

The cab door closed, and it sped off down the street.

August let go of my hand and walked to the front of the building. Silently, I followed him inside.

Sylvia's studio was the same size as Gary's, though it was a corner unit with windows all around. The studio I'd had there years ago was a quarter the size. There was a small kitchen area, a futon platform in the front corner, and a bathroom in the back corner. Beside the bathroom was a work area with an easel and a long table filled with rags, paint tubes and brushes. There was no table or chairs.

August's suitcase was open on the floor beside the bed, clothes spilling over the sides. His portfolio and camera bag were by the front door.

He took off his coat and dropped it on the camera bag.

"You want some tea?"

"Sure." I stood by the door. "Lot nicer than The Factory, eh? This must be eight hundred square feet."

August plugged the kettle in and turned around. "Yeah, it's big. You coming in or what?"

I closed the door and walked a few feet into the room. The old pine floors had been refinished to a high gloss shine and my footsteps echoed off the high ceilings.

I had never been more nervous in my life.

"So, when did you decide to shoot people again?"

August kept his back to me. "Around the same time you left."

"Your portraits are incredible."

"Thanks," August said. He braced his hands on the counter, his back stiff. "I had good subjects." He turned around quickly. "You can take your coat off if you want."

I undid a few buttons and stopped. "I will if you stop being angry."

"I'm not angry," he said, rubbing his arms.

"You sound like you are. You know why I left. Can you blame me?"

August thrust his hands in his front pockets. "No." He yanked his hands out. "Yes. You could have stuck around and let me figure things out. Shit, what am I saying? I knew you were going to leave. I knew from the second you set foot in Watson you were going to leave."

A trickle of sweat rolled down my back. I undid my coat and slipped it off, folded it over my arm and pressed it against my stomach.

August looked at me from under his lashes. "She wasn't pregnant. It was a mean stupid lie to make me feel guilty."

"I know."

August's head snapped up. "How?"

"Mia sent me a letter before Christmas."

He folded his lips in and nodded. "So you've known for awhile." He nodded his head again, then changed directions and shook it. "I guess that's not the point." He stopped and looked to the side. "I know why you came to Toronto. To get rid of... us."

I stared at him, blinking rapidly, trying to bring his words into focus.

"What happened between us is not something I can get rid of. Jesus." I stopped and swallowed the dryness in my throat. "It just felt like everything was falling apart."

August walked towards me and then stopped. "So you didn't...?"

I waited a moment for him to go on. When he didn't I prompted him. "I didn't..."

He sucked in his cheek and nodded his head. "You don't want me involved."

I looked away. "I'm leaving tomorrow."

"Yeah, I thought so."

"What?"

"I knew you weren't sticking around Toronto. Where are you going?"

"Vancouver."

August nodded. "You're flying?"

"Driving."

"By yourself?"

"Yes."

"You think that's a good idea?"

I didn't want to, but I smiled. "Jesus, you sound like my mother."

The kettle let out a shrill whistle.

August walked over to the counter. "You want peppermint or chamomile?"

A strange limbo happened in the next few hours. Everything unresolved just hung there between us, but we both ignored it and sat on the floor and drank tea and talked about photography.

I told August about my recent documenting of my body and my discovery of oleopasto.

"I'd really like to see them," he said as if we were friends who lived in the same town.

"Yeah, I'd like that," I said.

I looked around the room. The windows reflected the light

inside, squares of black onyx beyond which the city was still moving.

"I should get going," I said, getting up from the floor. I looked at my watch. It was just after two a.m.

August continued to sit on the floor, running his finger around the lip of his cup.

"I'm sorry for being angry before," he said. "I never wanted to hurt you. I just wanted you to find your joy."

The ache of regret filled my body in a fast rush. I had to leave now before I hesitated.

I put my coat on and walked to the door. August got up and followed me over. I bit the inside of my mouth hard, then turned around to face him.

"Well, hope the rest of your exhibit goes well."

"Thanks."

We stood a foot apart, the silence growing awkward.

I took a big breath. "Okay. Well..."

"Wait." August took hold of my arms. "Don't just leave."

"What do you want me to say?"

He tightened his hold on my arms. "Tell me you're happy. That you're better off without me."

I looked away and gave a nervous laugh. "August, this is crazy."

He shook me gently. "It's always been crazy. Maybe that's the way it's supposed to be."

"Don't."

"Albertine, there's a reason you came tonight. What's in the future?"

I stiffened. "Let's not talk about the future."

"Why not?"

"I don't want to."

August looked at me for a moment and released my arms. "Oh," he said, nodding his head. "You haven't decided."

"It's kind of a blur right now."

"Well, you must know something."

"I know I shouldn't have come tonight." I turned and put my

hand on the doorknob.

"You don't mean that." He spun me around and cupped my face in his hands. "I can feel it. Your skin's beating."

I opened my mouth to speak, but my words froze in my throat.

"Stop giving up on everything," he said.

Then he pulled me to him. As soon as his lips touched mine, I was lost. I'd forgotten how electric his kisses were. His arms slipped around me and my hands were in his hair, feeling the soft brush on the back of his neck, the heat pulsing from the tendons above his spine. His tongue touched the inside of my lip and I felt the crazy want explode inside me.

I tore myself away. "I've gotta go." I grabbed frantically for the doorknob.

August didn't try to stop me when I stumbled out the door and ran down the hallway.

For twenty-four hours after leaving August, my life hung in the balance. Every time I thought about him saying, *stop giving up on everything*, the urge to fight tightened like a muscle inside me. I didn't want to run away. Not this time. If I was ever going to find the balance, I had to leave unfettered.

God, I wish he hadn't kissed me.

The following day, I packed the van at dawn, said goodbye to my mother and drove downtown under the blue-black sky to Richmond and Bathurst.

Gary had given me the security code for the building and I let myself in, carrying my portfolio with my recent prints.

When August opened the door, he was dressed and looked like he'd been up for hours. He also looked like he'd been expecting me.

"You want some coffee?" he said. He noticed the portfolio. "Are those your photographs?" He took the portfolio from me and motioned me into the studio.

He acted as if nothing weird had happened the night before last. We drank coffee, sitting on the floor, while the sun inched across the hardwood in wide bands of gold.

"I'm supposed to be on my way to Vancouver right now," I said.

"Really," August said. He drank his coffee.

"I said goodbye to my mother."

August watched my face. "That must have been hard. What about your father?"

"He died nine years ago."

"Was he sick?"

"He was struck by lightning."

August's eyes widened, but he said nothing for a moment. He got up from the floor and took his empty coffee cup to the sink. "I'm glad I never knew my mother or father," he said. "I never had to say goodbye or have them die."

"Didn't you ever want to find your mother?"

August turned around. "No. Why would I? She gave me away. Parents aren't supposed to give their kids away."

I shivered and got up from the floor. "I need to use your bathroom."

"Sure." He pointed to the back corner.

When I came out of the bathroom a few minutes later, August was sitting on the floor again, my portfolio leaning against his knees.

"So let's see your oleopasta."

I laughed. "It's oleo-pas-to."

"Right," he said.

I sat down across from him and he slid the portfolio over to me. I unzipped the case. I'd mounted the prints, but hadn't titled them yet. Usually the titles came to me as soon as I saw the developed prints, but for some reason I got stuck naming my own body.

"These aren't in any particular order," I said, handing him the first one, a shot of my left hand.

August looked at the print and nodded.

I handed him one of my feet and another of my arm.

He got up, took the three prints to the kitchen and lined them up against the bottom cupboards, then stood back to look.

"More," he said, coming back to where I was kneeling on the floor.

I handed him the next three, a leg, an eye and a mouth, and he nodded, then took them over to the cupboards and added to the line.

I was sweating inside my heavy sweater. August came back and stood over me. I handed him the photo of my torso.

He looked at it, but this time he didn't nod.

I handed him the next one, but he kept looking at the torso. Finally, he put it down on the floor and took the next photo, a shot of my thigh, then one of my ear, and another of my neck. He took the last three and lined them up against the cupboards, then came back for the torso shot, holding it out in front of him for a moment. He went back to the kitchen, parted the line of photos in the middle and slipped the torso shot in.

Starting from the left he'd ordered them: feet, arm, hand, ear, neck, torso, eye, mouth, thigh, leg.

He came back and knelt on the floor, facing the cupboards. "These are beautiful. They're not who you are, they're *what* you are. It's like looking at an x-ray. You can see under the surface of your skin." He fell silent, staring at the row of photos, rubbing the web of his hand between his fingers. "Are there any more?" he said, turning to me.

"That's it."

"What's that one?" he said, pointing to the print left in my portfolio.

"It's something else. It doesn't go with this series."

"Let me see it anyway."

I shook my head and pulled the portfolio towards me.

"Come on, Albertine."

I pulled the print out and handed it to him.

August held it out. "Oh," he said.

It was the photograph I'd done of August. I'd mounted it and titled it with the intention of putting together a series of portraits.

"Soul Of A Man," August said. He sniffed through his nose and let go of one side of the print to rub his knuckle across his eye. "I remember that day. I kissed you and freaked you out. It was right before I went to Ottawa. And I kissed you again at the train station." August released a laugh and kept looking at the photograph. "I figured you'd be gone by the time I got back."

"Guess I fooled you," I said.

"No," he said and got up from the floor, carrying the photo to the kitchen.

He stood for a minute looking at the print in his hand and the ones lined up against the cupboards. Then he picked out the print of my torso and carried it and Soul Of A Man back to where I was sitting.

He knelt down in front of me and turned the prints around facing me.

"This is our future."

"Photography?"

"No. You're not looking hard enough."

I looked at the photos, my silvery torso and August's sad and wistful face. The connection between the two created a third imaginary picture. It was there in my shining skin and deep in August's eyes, a portent of the future.

I shook my head. August didn't have the whole picture. He didn't know everything.

He didn't press it any further and laid the photos down on the floor. "Do you have a print of that photograph?"

"What photograph?"

"The one you went to court for."

I shook my head. There was a hollow sadness building inside me.

"Is it something you don't like to look at anymore?" August said.

I got up from the floor, anxious to move. "I can't look at it anymore. It doesn't exist."

August got up. "What do you mean?"

I closed my eyes and saw red stars floating on the backs of my eyelids. "The negative was destroyed."

"You're kidding." He touched my arm. "I'm really sorry."

There was a buffer of heat between our bodies. I could smell the shampoo he'd used, an apple scent, and the clean soapy smell of his shaving cream. I wanted to touch him, but the way he was looking at me hurt. I knew he understood. "She burned everything," I said.

"Why did she do it?" he said.

"She hated it. Thought it was offensive. Shit, everyone thought it was offensive."

"Did you?"

I shook my head. "I thought it was beau–" My throat choked on the rest of the word.

"They didn't like the photograph, Albertine. Doesn't mean they didn't like you."

"Yeah, it does. I took the picture. It didn't take itself. I made them pose that way."

August shook his head. "You saw what was there. They saw what wasn't there. The camera doesn't lie, Albertine. You should know that."

I looked at the prints lying on the floor, my torso rising up from the paper, the round white orb of August's face. "Yeah, I know that now."

He looked like he was about to say something more, but changed his mind. He picked up my empty coffee cup from the floor and took it into the kitchen. He looked at the prints lined up against the cupboards for a moment. "You said you were heading out of town."

I blinked, confused by the abrupt shift in gears. "Yeah, I was."

"You should go."

"Wait. What?"

August shook his head and smiled. "You're a great photographer, Albertine. That's what you need to do. Go pursue it."

I folded my arms around my middle and pressed hard. "I don't know what I need. I need peace. I need sanity. I need everything to stop being so hard." A band of steel tightened in my head.

August walked over and stood in front of me. "Then what are you doing here? You should go. You don't need me."

"I can't. My life still feels like a mess. I need to figure it out. I lost everything because of that photograph. I moved to Watson to start over. Except... I fucked it up again. I lied about who I was. I got involved with you when I shouldn't have. God, that was stupid. You have no idea how stupid."

August grabbed my face in his hands and held me still. "Stop."

Tears popped out of my eyes and ran down my face. "I'm so sorry."

I bit my bottom lip, holding back from really crying.

August looked at my mouth for a second. "Don't be sorry," he said, then pressed his lips against my lips and held them there.

Everything went calm, like the wind had been sucked out of my storm. August moved his lips against my mouth, and I followed and let him really kiss me.

He was so wrong. I did need him. I needed him like he was oxygen or food.

It took a minute before I felt him let go. He pulled my sweater over my head and pressed his face into my neck, my hair, kissing areas of skin like he was christening me.

"Don't ever be sorry," he said into my shoulder, tightening his arms around me.

We made love desperately, with aching in every kiss, reluctant to let go for even a second. It was like we both knew it would be the last time. The problem was, once it was over, we couldn't stop. We made love again and again while the sun shifted positions around the room. We didn't talk. The only sounds were our sighs and the waves of our breaths, rising and crashing over and over again.

I couldn't get enough of him. As soon as we moved apart, I wanted to be joined to him again. It was like some kind of fever, a craziness that possessed me.

When we had exhausted ourselves, I slept for a while in his arms. His hands were cupped around my face, the tenderness of his touch still surprising after hours of familiarizing myself with the way he loved.

When I woke up, it was dawn again. August was gone. I rolled over in the tangled sheets that had the funk of love, and looked across the room. His suitcase was gone and so was his camera bag and portfolio. I sat up quickly. The light from the kitchen shone across the floor. My photos and my portfolio were gone, too.

I put my clothes on in a panic, my head throbbing with fear. I sat down on the bed again after I was dressed. I had no idea what to do.

When I shoved my hands in my coat pockets and discovered the keys to the van were gone, the room went fuzzy for a moment, and then I jumped up and ran.

I ran down four flights of stairs. The cold air hit my face when I opened the front door of the building and I sucked in a lungful. The sky was streaked with pale stripes of indigo, orange and black. The streets were empty and in the distance I heard the rolling thunder of a streetcar. I looked down the street at the row of dark cars. A plume of exhaust rose from between them. It was my van, idling in the dark.

A dark figure was sitting behind the wheel, his head down reading something spread across the steering wheel. I walked around to the driver's side door and yanked it open.

"What the hell are you doing?" I was yelling, the blood pounding in my face.

August had a map bunched in his hands. "Jesus, you scared the shit out of me," he said breathlessly. "I'm driving you to Vancouver. Just checking the map." He folded the edges of the map and put it on the floor between the seats.

"You're what?" I said, backing up. "Get out."

He started to slide out of the seat, then stopped with his foot on the running board and shook his head. "Get in," he said.

The cold was working its way inside my boots. I'd been in too much of a hurry to put my socks on. I walked around to the passenger side, opened the door and climbed in.

August closed his door and we sat in silence while the van idled roughly, the heater rattling full blast. There was a thin pattern of frost on the windshield, and the dark street looked like it was behind a lace curtain.

I reached over and turned the heater down and it was quiet.

"You took my portfolio," I said.

"I packed it," August said.

"What the hell are you doing?"

"I told you. I'm driving you to Vancouver."

"What about your show?"

He shrugged. "It's only running for two more days. After that, I don't have another one booked till April."

"Where?"

He smiled and rubbed his mouth. "Vancouver."

"Bullshit."

He turned to me. "Seriously. In Tsawwassen. At the reservation. They liked that photo you did of me, and when they found out I was a photographer, they offered me a show."

I closed my eyes and felt the world tilting crazily. It was like it had all been worked out ahead of time, my future planned to intersect with his. No, it didn't feel right.

August was watching me. "You can't drive all the way there by yourself."

"Yeah, I can," I said. My heart was beating so hard I thought I might bust something. "What are you going to do after you've driven me there? Go all the way back home?"

He nodded. "Yeah, probably. Or maybe I'll stick around till my show and go back after it's over. So you ready to go?"

I hated him for being so calm. I felt like a raving psycho in comparison. My hands were shaking and there was a tremor in the skin on my stomach. I'd gotten used to the idea of doing this alone, had steeled myself for it. If I opened the door a crack, it was going to blow all the way open and let in dependence and need.

"I don't think I can do this," I said, bending over and hugging my knees.

"I know you don't," August said quietly. "Just let go and have a little faith."

He put the van in gear, and we pulled away from the curb, moving into the sunrise. When we turned south towards the lake to get on the highway, the water shone like liquid tar, a band of black turning to deep blue like the color of August's eyes.

We drove straight through to Thunder Bay, only stopping to switch places. August drove, I slept. I drove, August slept. It kept conversation to a minimum.

I kept myself in the moment. I had to. Our departure from Toronto had been so abrupt, I still couldn't acknowledge that my plans had changed. August was only driving me there. I'd get there sooner. And then?

When we crossed the border into Manitoba, the prairies stretched out before us and reality began to sink in. We'd left Ontario. It was too late for August to go back. The past was unspooling in the rearview mirror while I tried to root myself in the present. It wasn't working. After a few hours of endless flat blacktop I was going nuts not talking about the future.

When we stopped to get gas, I couldn't avoid it any longer. I owed August some knowledge of what lay ahead. It did involve him.

We parked beside the gas station and stood outside the van stretching our legs. It had been mild and sunny most of the day, but now a soft snow was floating down from the darkening sky. I watched it fall on August's hair and pictured him as an old man, gray and mighty.

"August, there's something I have to tell you."

He looked at the trees behind the gas station.

"I'm going to have a baby."

He kept looking at the trees.

"Aren't you going to say anything?"

He shook his head.

"Don't you want to know whose it is?"

He turned his head and looked at me. "It's mine."

"Boy, you seem pretty certain."

He walked over to me and laid his hand over my stomach. "When you left and went to Toronto I thought it was because you were getting rid of it."

"What?"

He pressed my stomach. "The baby."

"What are you saying?"

"I figured you'd made a decision and that's why you left."

There was a tingling sensation in my jaw. "Are you saying you knew?"

"Of course I knew. I've been waiting for you to tell me."

"I just found out. How the hell did you know?"

"I've known all along. I knew the night it happened. After the party."

I moved away from him. "It could have been sometime after that."

August shook his head. "No, it was that night in the forest. I knew the second it happened." He frowned and rubbed his forehead. "I thought it was planned."

"What?" The word came out so fast it was a wheeze. "It was an accident. I didn't think I could get pregnant. I had pelvic inflammatory disease when I was twenty and the doctor told me I wouldn't be able to have kids. It was an accident."

August was looking at me funny. "It wasn't an accident. It was meant to happen that night otherwise we wouldn't have made love."

"You're saying we only had sex so I could get pregnant?"

"We didn't have *sex*, Albertine."

"Oh, Jesus. That's why you're here. I didn't say you needed to be involved in this. Don't do this 'cause you feel responsible. I'll do just fine on my own." I backed further away from him.

He moved closer. "We're both her parents, Albertine. There's nothing that will ever change that."

A truck sped by, hitting a slushy pothole with a loud whoosh. A shiver snaked down my back. "Her?"

August shoved his hands in his pockets and kicked at a hump of ice. "Yeah. It's a girl and I think we should name her Aurora."

"Oh my god, you've already picked out a name."

He kept looking at the ground. "Yeah. In Roman mythology, Aurora was the goddess of the dawn. That's when we made her... at dawn."

I tried to swallow, but my throat was full. I felt everything slipping away from me, beyond my control.

"I don't think I can do this," I said, getting into the van.

August walked around to the driver's side and got in. He closed the door and sat with his hands on the steering wheel. "Yes, you can. Just let go and have some faith."

We didn't talk for hours after that. I couldn't let go. The only thing I had faith in was my ability to survive on my own. If I let go, my life would no longer be my own. I couldn't accept that this was meant to happen. The future was supposed to hold surprises, good things to be anticipated, and the possibility of bad stuff was what kept you strong. If I let go, I would give into weakness and just let things happen. I'd already done that. I'd moved to Watson broken and weak and let myself be carried into a nest of lies. I vowed to never do that again.

What did August want? A child? A new link in his immortality? Was it simply a need for a family to erase the ache of being an orphan?

As we neared Winnipeg, I asked him. "If Caroline were really pregnant would you have stayed with her in Watson?"

"No," he said. "And if I'd really thought about it at the time I would have known she was lying. I couldn't have a child with Caroline. We never made love."

"Pardon?"

"Babies come from love, Albertine. Not sex. Caroline and I had sex. You and I... that was something different."

"So you're saying it was fate."

"It was timing."

"So we were meant to be together so we could make a baby? Jesus, how can you accept that? Don't you ever question anything?"

August sighed. "Albertine, you know what your problem is? You question things too much. You question them to death. What the hell are you so afraid of?"

I fell asleep making a list of everything I was afraid of. It got so long, it unraveled into my dreams and I got tangled up in a mess of doubts.

I woke up when we stopped moving.

"I can't drive anymore," August said, rubbing his eyes.

We switched places and drove on into the night. August laid his head back, and when I looked over a few times his eyes were closed.

A few miles later, when I thought he was asleep, he spoke. "My mother didn't want me and I don't know if my father even knew about me. I'm the product of sex, Albertine. The random, unfortunate one that got through."

I drove on through the dark, feeling my belly expanding, the road blurring as August's words rose again and again in my ears and I had to blink away the pain of his fractured heart.

We didn't talk about the future for the next two days as we sped across the flatness of Saskatchewan and Alberta, and up into the Rocky Mountains. We didn't talk about the past either. Our conversations had to do with food and stopping for gas.

August had retreated into a closed shroud of thought. I was afraid to ask him what he was thinking. I was questioning every one of his actions since we'd made love that first time and wondering if everything he'd said or done was because he knew I was pregnant.

When we reached Banff, we decided to check into a hotel. After two days of silence in a confined space, August seemed relieved to be more than a few feet away from me.

It was a pretty hotel, set in the mountains overlooking a ski resort. August brought our bags and portfolios in from the van and while he ordered room service, I took a shower.

When I came out of the bathroom, the food was there. August had turned off the lights and opened the curtains and stood in front of the window looking at the twinkling light on the ski hill. He still had his jacket on.

The hotel robe was too big and I tied the belt tighter and took the room service tray and put it on the bed. There was a plate of pasta, a bowl of ice cream and a large glass of milk. "Aren't you eating?" I said.

August kept looking out the window. "I just want to know her."

"I know."

"I hoped I could talk you into letting me stick around on the drive." He turned around. "I figured I had three or four days to state my case. Only–" He let out a breath and tilted his head back. "I didn't take into account you might have already made up your mind."

"I never said–"

"I just want to know her."

"Yeah, I know. But that's not a good reason for us to be together."

August looked at me. "You think I don't think about the future? There are no guarantees. You can't ask for them."

"Yes, but I don't want to be together just because of the baby."

"And that's all it would be for you."

"I didn't say that."

He walked over to the bed and sat down, slipping out of his jacket. "You can't make decisions based on what might happen, Albertine. There's no way to know. I accept the future whatever it's going to be. All you can do is wish… make predictions. This baby is a prediction on our future."

"You believe in predictions. I don't know if I do. Besides, you yourself said I don't need you."

His head jerked and he got up from the bed and walked over to the window. "You don't think…" He stopped and ran his hand through his hair. "You think I don't…"

"Please complete a sentence," I said.

He took a breath and came back over to the bed, then crawled on his hands and knees, pushing the tray aside until he was leaning over me. "I believe the future brought us this baby so we can be together."

I looked away.

August sat back on his legs. "Albertine I know you wanted me once. What's changed?"

"This baby," I said, touching my stomach.

"Do you love me?"

"What? I can't answer that."

"Why not? You don't know, or you're afraid to tell me you don't?"

"What difference does it make?" My throat swelled with pain and when I tried to hold it back, a tremor started around my mouth and my eyes filled with hot tears.

I heard August suck in a breath. "Is that what the problem is? You think I don't love you? You think I don't love you so much my heart broke when you left?" He took my hands and pulled me towards him. "I'm not just here because of Aurora, Albertine. I know you don't need me. But do you want me?"

I moved over to him and put my arms around his neck, burying my face in the collar of his shirt. "Yes. And I hate that you're so certain about everything."

His muscles tightened under my arms. "I have to be."

"What if it doesn't work out?"

August pulled back and looked in my face. "What if it does?"

"I knew I was doomed the first time I saw you."

"Me too. You changed my life, Albertine."

"You got mine back."

I felt him shiver, then his arms tightened around me.

After he fell asleep, I got up and opened his portfolio. Sure enough, inside, he had two of my prints, the one of my torso and Soul Of A Man. I lined them up at the end of the bed and sat on the floor looking at them. Then I looked through his portfolio again and found the print he'd done of me. I pulled it out and lined it up beside the other two. Aurora Borealis. He'd named the photograph not for me, but for the baby, for the future. He had known.

I crawled back into bed and curled up beside him. I slid my arms around him, and he stirred in his sleep. The moon shone through the window. A band of silver light touched his face. I could see his soul. I wanted to hold it for just a breath of time.

EPILOGUE

Mightier Than Swords

Today is Aurora's tenth birthday. August and I are giving her, her first camera. It may be genetics or the fact that she's always been around cameras, but she wants to be a photographer. Even as a baby she had a keen awareness of the camera and loved having her picture taken. She'd go still and stare into the lens patiently until the shutter clicked. At five, she could pose like a professional model, looking serious and introspective.

Lately, she likes to borrow my old Leica or August's spare Nikon and shoot playgrounds around our neighborhood, but is adamant that there are no children in the shots. She takes haunting photos of empty slides and abandoned swings. When I asked her why she didn't want any kids in the shots she said, "You're supposed to imagine them playing, not see them playing." I worry about her flair for the dramatic, but I'm also fascinated by the trajectory of her imagination.

I'm feeling introspective today. It may be turning forty and the need to look back and trace my own trajectory. I'm still working for Exit magazine, doing some art stuff on the side, and I have a show every couple of years.

August's portrait business is steady and when he has a client over to his studio, he reminds me of my grandfather, the way he charms people into giving their best pose. He also teaches photography to teenagers at the Tsawwassen Reservation. Even though he is Ojibwe, they have embraced him as their own and some of his photographs hang in the Tswwassen gallery as part of their permanent collection.

I looked at him this morning while he was still sleeping and was jolted by the fact that he is still here. I don't know if he has accepted the future so thoroughly that the will to change is gone, or if the future has accepted him and bends with him, like a strong tree.

For the past ten years, I have given him a clock for his birthday so he can continue to commune with time and the seconds going by. The clocks tick in varied syncopations, rhumbas and shuffles, polkas and waltzes. People have asked me if the ticking drives me crazy. I don't think I could stand the silence. I need the heartbeat of time to keep me grounded. August is soothed by the sound. I've found him in the middle of the night sitting in the living room, rocking to the rhythms with his eyes closed and a smile on his lips.

Our first few years together weren't easy. While I had worried that August would leave, it was I who left. It was after Aurora was born and I wanted to get back to work. We were living on Bowen Island and I needed to be in the city. August didn't want to go. So I left him and Aurora and moved back to Vancouver. It lasted six weeks. August showed up one day with Aurora in his arms. "I don't care where we live," he said. "We both need to be with you." It took me a long time to get over the guilt of leaving Aurora. In the six weeks I was without them, I cried most of the time and the ache of loneliness made every breath painful. I thought I could survive alone. I couldn't. I needed them both like oxygen and food. It was a hard lesson.

We were broke much of the time and lived in some questionable neighborhoods and sometimes I wondered if it would ever stop being so hard. But, on Aurora's first day of school, the sun broke over the water and I realized somewhere inside me had been the strength and faith to keep pushing through, and August and I were no longer fighting the constant pull of gravity. The years had knitted us together. At this point I couldn't live without him.

When I look at Aurora, I see August. She looks so much like him,

I've yet to find any physical traits she may have inherited from me. Her mannerisms are so August-like, the slow way she talks and the graceful way she moves. Her long black hair and peach-tea skin hint at her Ojibwe blood, but her blue eyes are the accident of August's birth. And despite what he said about being the random unfortunate one that got through, I think August's capacity for love is so big, he was determined to be conceived despite the lack of love between his parents.

Aurora will never know that sadness. She is loved. And despite the fulfillment that both August and I have in our careers, she is our best creation.

August was right. Aurora is our prediction on the future. I watch her grow and inside her innocence are tokens that remind us to treasure our own purity. I picture her children and grandchildren and it allows me to keep hoping. Her presence confirms August's belief. She was conceived at the right moment. It was meant to happen. We came together that night because she needed to be made and August and I needed the future to bring us together.

August hasn't changed much and that in itself amazes me. I've waited for boredom or disappointment to dull the shine of his spirit. It hasn't.

He has maintained his purity for thirty-nine years. That is a miracle. I look at the photograph I took of him and see his soul. I look at him today and it is still there, right on the surface, unprotected, shimmering and delicate, yet stronger than armor, mightier than the swords of the critics, unbowed by the hatred that surrounds us in this world, blown with beauty, unbroken by time.